Buckskin Cocaine

Erika T. Wurth

Astrophil Press
at University of South Dakota
2017

Copyright © 2016 by Erika T. Wurth
Cover art by Douglas Miles
Layout and design by duncan b. barlow
Additional proofreading provided by Cheyenne Marco

Astrophil Press at University of South Dakota
1st pressing 2017

Library of Congress Cataloging-in-Publication Data
Erika T. Wurth 1975
Buckskin Cocaine/Erika Wurth
     p. cm.
  ISBN 978-0-9822252-7-1 (pbk. : paper)
  1.Fiction, American
Library of Congress Control Number: 2017940868

http://www.astrophilpress.com

Table of Contents

Barry Four Voices

BECAUSE I'M FAMOUS because I'm rich because I grew up poor on a reservation and that's what no one understands even though I have been telling the same story, over and over for years, to anyone who would listen. Because I was an alcoholic because I deserve to get what I want because I do get what I want because I work harder than everyone else. Because I know how to shake like I'm laughing, my long, angry body turned away from the faces floating in front of me. Because I know how to fake it. Because there is a way I'm not faking it. Because I do love my life my wife my children and that's what makes me a good person. I'm happy. Because I'm very happy.

Because people are after me, after all. They are and they always have been and they always will be. And no one understands. No matter how many times I tell the story, I like telling the story, you'd think I'd be sick of my own story, but I'm not. I have to tell it and when I do, I will look at the faces floating in front of me like they are a great big breast, and I am desperate for milk.

And when one of the men who lives inside of me does things, that man who is really who I am *but quiet I don't talk about that* it is OK because that man needs to eat. He's hungry, he's hungrier than I am and if he doesn't eat, he will kill me. Because there are ways in which I'm already dead, not from the things I experienced as a child *because everyone has hope when they are young don't they* but because of the things I cannot help but do. I said that I do these things so that he won't kill me but I also said that I have been dead for years, which I have, I have, I have, I should be happy.

I tell myself that I feel love but people like me don't feel things like love. Do they? When I look at my boys my eyes fill with tears sometimes but it is because I see myself and I feel sorry for myself, so sorry for myself I feel like punching myself or someone I almost love as hard as I've ever punched anything like when I used to drink and even the trees made me rage and cry and when I would wake up in the hospital or my friend's house or my house or a strange house or did that happen or have I made up another story so that I can create food for him to eat and eat and eat.

Because because because I am an artist I am an Indian I am a man because I am sick because I'm smarter than most people because she was a slut and that's what they want, with their little blue skirts and their little blue shoes. *God why can't they feel shame?* Because underneath all of this and above it and inside it I am a good person. In fact I am the best, because I hate myself.

One of the men inside me believes that the women are all white, but they aren't. I know that they're not but when on the rare occasion I let myself talk to myself, to the one who lives on top of the other one that's most on top, I can see through his cold black eyes all of their brown or yellow-brown hands, their look of love, their faces their fucking, fucking faces. They're anyone who loves me, even just a little, even for the wrong reasons because all of the reasons are wrong, are right. Because I am always right.

Sometimes I tell myself, or the man who might eat me, that they're all the same woman, white or brown, whichever hips are in my long hands late at night after the words have been vomited up, one by one, the faces like a nightmare I tell myself that I will never wake from even though it is a dream come true, true, true, I'm very happy, he says, the knife so close to my throat.

Sometimes I tell the faces floating in front of me that I want to love other men so that they will never see the truth, which is that everything I touch I burn, I burn for, I burn up. But then again, I tell the faces so many things. After all, they need to eat too. The truth is that it is not even about my father, perhaps it is about my mother, I stopped wanting to really know a long time ago. Fire is only a metaphor for me now.

I make a lot of jokes about my death and dying to show how unafraid I am but that is another lie the men inside me make rise up, everyone will get a Pendleton. They call all of the boys that will come after me young guns but these are boys who maybe have never held a gun. Neither have I but when I lie about it, I am filled with rage, the hate choking me up, the sadness, I need to sleep, he's made me so tired, they all have.

There are times when I laugh with my wife over a small thing, and for a moment I let one of the men out while the knife twists hard in my gut. Maybe he doesn't love her, but he pities her, or maybe he can at least say he understands her and wants her to be happy, remembers the hope he felt when he was let out long enough to rope her in *before the blood came out.* And then the one with the knife comes and the one who is let out only for strangers and small, good moments is pushed down. He is so small. I pity him. He thinks he's more real than the rest of us, but he has to think that or he will die.

In the end there is the tunnel where the wind blows, and it is clean; the rage is there and the need, and my entire collection of knives, and they are beautiful, shining in the long, silver tunnel that whistles with the loneliness of love. And there is the rope that I used to bring my wife to me, and though I hang the both of us with it, over and over because of what happened, but not because of what happened, I am like a dying animal gone mad from the smell of itself, somehow the knives that are there to remind me that I could die at any time are also the knives that free us both from that animal that has been waiting to tear me apart since I was born.

All the littlest man wants is to be pulled away from the rest of the men, the rage, the women, the wife, the boys, the faces floating under the lights, the words I write with the man underneath who lives with his knife at my throat. He wants something beautiful, pure. He wants the tunnel to collapse but the tunnel is a bad good, it's a place where the men run free, where I keep the knives, where the rage is so clean and pure and like fire that no matter how hot it burns it can't burn me up, I can't escape it. It is like the den of that dying animal, and it has been abused all of its life and is only alive long enough to hate more. Getting away would be like death, a clean, lovely thing, like when I was young and I could look around at the reservation, the people I had come not to trust at a distance, but they were beautiful anyway, my mother somewhere waiting to put me in her arms. But I am pulled back. By the rope, by the women, the knives, into the tunnel. By the blood. I do not understand what purgatory means.

Sometimes I comfort myself with the little things, and then I talk about them, and then I tell people who I could never be close to how much I love them, and they sigh, and the man with the knife at my throat likes this, he likes it a lot because it makes me feel like I'm still alive and breathing and maybe have all kinds of love to give and to get and to hold. I do. Have all kinds of love. At least one of the men inside me does. He told me so once, in a dream.

When I am about to go to sleep is when it's the worst. I think this is when it's the worst for everyone, when we jerk awake and feel a kind of deep pain that seems like truth but is probably fear. The kind of fear that we felt before words came into our lives, the kind of fear that we had when we were young, when we were babies. When we're in that moment of almost sleep, our limbs hurt and we have to work hard to push all of the men away because it's then that we understand that they are all holding knives, and we are too.

There are times when people laugh at the words and I hate them for it, I make that clear by staring at the floating faces until they are silent. But I can't stand their silence either. But I made them laugh, I know it, I made the food, I made the man, I gave him the knife, long ago, in a dream I had as a child. It was my favorite dream, because it gave me power.

What makes me angriest is when people dare to take my truth away, like they know it, like they have a man at their throats, like they've seen the blood that I've seen, I'm very happy. I have the truth. No one knows it like I do, like the men do, I've worked very hard, harder than anyone else, and I have taken a shovel to stiff, hard ground for years and after years and years of my back breaking, breaking in half I have uncovered something. It is my face.

What still surprises me is when people try to push at the men. They're always going to be stronger, because I can wander the streets at night while my wife sleeps and my boys sleep and love everyone I see from a distance because I'm very smart. That's what the man tells me, and I believe him, because though I now know that I was born with him with his knife at my throat he has never pushed in, I'm a survivor.

I'm growing, I think, still, the men inside me are louder, I know that and I think it's a good thing, because when they finally take over I can stop trying, I can stop being in pain, I'm sure of that, the little white and yellow and pink pills they're everywhere, oh God I'm so tired please let the knife push in. What scares me so much isn't death anymore it's that maybe I can't die, I'm a survivor. That word is very important to me.

What the littlest man doesn't seem to remember is that he was the one in control when I was a baby, doesn't he remember how weak we were back then? When everyone had fists on us, everyone had their knives at our throats, that's when the men I was born with first came out, they taught me so much but I still wonder if the littlest man will get out because sometimes I can feel him staring at something I want to love through my eyes and I think *God no,* I'm very happy. And then the words come out again, and it is OK. But I'm scared that the littlest man will get out. I don't even know if he has a knife. Dear God, what does he have? What will he eat?

And when I think about my wife all I really think about is guilt, about what she sits in the place of because she doesn't really exist, none of us do, or at least that's what I told myself when all I wanted was for the blood to stop coming out of her, not because she was real, but because the man with the knife was whispering, *look, there's another man that is another you that could be pure coming out of that thing,* that thing, that thing that is just like all of the other things that love me, for the right or wrong reasons.

The man with the knife likes me to laugh, it's because then he knows I'm nervous and honestly I'm nervous all the time but I'm very happy, so it's OK. I laugh when the hate is in my throat, when someone has tried to take the truth away, and one of the men has punished them for it. It's funniest when they don't even know it's coming. But they deserve it, and even if they didn't, the man with the knife must eat. It's me or them. Somebody has to be punished for their sins, for mine. It's me or them, and I'm a survivor, "I'm a very happy, happy, happy, survivor."

O God the world is so full of color and that's why I must think in black and white, why I must tell everyone about how dangerous and complicated the words are when I know they make people feel such simple things but my God it's not my fault first of all it's the floating face's fault, the women's fault, they make me feel so much rage and I tell myself that I'm the littlest man feeling for everyone else but even the littlest man inside of all of the men, the one all of the men push down, he feels, he feels so much, but only for himself.

This is the difference between empathy and sensitivity. *Do you understand now?* No one understands, which is why the man with the knife is always so busy punishing them, don't they understand that it's me or them? How many times do I have to tell my story?

Candy Francois

THERE ARE SO MANY GORGEOUS PHOTOS OF ME. And I'm beautiful in every one of them; thin, perfect, frozen in time. And the drugs were lovely. They were like ice-skating with your best friend when you were eight, like falling in love, like living on cake. I was in New York for six years in a loft in the West Village when I first met George. George...that womanizing, shitty filmmaker. I had a wonderful life; I lived with a ton of other artists, though I was the only Native American. That made me unique. When I wasn't modeling, I was doing promotional work for clubs (that part was my favorite because they would have us dress up so crazy) but then sometimes I'd get a buckskin gig for a Native magazine, my face all stoic and my body covered in beads and leather on the cover, and that would be wonderful. I would send a copy to mom, who would send a copy to grandma, and they would write me and tell me how beautiful I was but when was I going to settle down? I thought the answer to that was never. Because getting older wasn't real, it wasn't something I ever thought about, it didn't even exist. I was in my early twenties, I was a model, I lived in New York.

I was dating a senator for a while there when I was twenty-two. A fucking senator. He was married. I had to keep it quiet. But the things he bought me. And we did so much blow. My friends loved him, because he would come to our apartment smelling of money and beauty and roll out the expensive drugs and take us all to dinner. And let me tell you how much he loved for me to put on the black leather gear I'd gotten from some of those club gigs, and whip his white, white ass. I loved it too. I loved everything about that time. My life was so glamorous and trashy and lovely and I was drunk and high and I felt like a rock star, like I was living inside of a neon light, like I was a god. I was in my early twenties, I was a model, I lived in New York.

The first time I met George, I'd just come from a shoot in Paris. I remember walking around that golden city filled with such an intense feeling of euphoria it was sexual; thin, dressed in a Christian Dior suit, my dyed black hair down to my ass, the men in that city practically falling all over themselves for la belle amérindienne and me strutting past and laughing on my way to meet some actor and director friends at a hip new restaurant. I'd been given a bit part in a little film and it was premiering at Red Stick in Santa Fe and I was ecstatic. I was sure that I would make it into film. Much as I loved dressing up for my buckskin gigs, or for powwow or ceremony for that matter, I was happy to play anything. I could pass for a lot of ethnicities. I'd even dyed my hair blonde once. And this was my first part in a movie and it had been a long time coming. I'd been auditioning for years. I'd told myself that struggle was part of it. That it was all about courage, about not giving up. When I'd audition, they'd get this really excited look when I'd come in. But when I'd read, that look would fade and I would leave feeling more and more defeated and depressed every time. I didn't understand. I'd taken a ton of classes at the New School. I figured that modeling was a lot like acting. You had to act when you modeled, you had to have presence. And I did. Everyone said I looked like I was about to go through the camera and eat whoever was on the other side. But modeling had been easy to break into. I told myself that the acting world was more complicated, more competitive. That it was only a matter of time. I was in my early twenties, I was a model, I lived in New York.

I was at a party after the premier in Santa Fe when one of my friends elbowed me and pointed in the direction of a fat little Navajo guy. *That's George Bull,* she said. *And?* I said. *He's a director.* I eyed him and he took it as some kind of cue to come up and start talking to me. I was irritated because I hate it when gross men think that they have the right to hit on me. He asked my name. I asked his, and he shook my hand with one of his wet little paws. He was quick to tell me that his film had premiered at Sundance. His friend Robert was right behind him and after a while it was clear that those two went around together like a married couple. Later I found out that Robert's film had premiered at Sundance too. And that it did a lot better than George's. Robert stared at me all bug eyed and silent and drank the PBRs that he'd brought and George kept going on and on about how important he was until I became bored. But I knew that I had to play nice, so I acted flirtatious, like what he was saying was entertaining. Though I wanted to strangle his fat little neck when he said something about my friend Sheena being nothing but a pretty little cunt. I'm sure it was because she didn't want to fuck him. He told me that I'd played a really good vampire and his little wife Robert snorted drink out of his nose and took off towards the bathroom. *Don't mind him,* George said and I nodded, though I disliked him even more. I did, however, let him have my phone number right before he left with Robert as I knew he was a potentially important connection. Robert had been whining, *Can't we goooo?* in-between gulps of PBR like a six year old nearly all night. George texted me for hours. I just kept texting *lol* back. He seemed to like that. Then I went home with this beautiful Cree actor from Canada who was in another film that was premiering at Red Stick. I wondered the next day if I should have been nicer but after a couple of weeks it was like *fuck that guy* because after the first film, I got another bit part and then later another, both with low budget Native productions. For a while, I started to believe that things were really happening. But I was never given any lines — or very few. And it kept landing me right back at Red Stick. And George was always there. Always trying to fuck me. And I would nod and flirt and text him back and go home with someone beautiful. That's the most humiliating part about it, that for years I brushed him away like he was an insect, like he was something I'd stepped on with one of my LaBoutin heels. Also, I'm Ojibwe and Cree. I practically dwarf that fucker. And he must have thought I was a moron. I found out pretty quickly that he only did Navajo films, cast Navajo actors. But he liked to find women like me, mixed woman, tall women, and indicate that he might cast them, and then fuck them and move onto the next. Please. I'd been using people for years in New York. I knew what it looked like from both sides. If I was going to fuck someone, it was because I was either going to get something from them or because I really actually wanted to fuck them. I was in my early twenties, I was a model, I lived in New York.

One night in New York, after I'd been feeling unusually tired and had just had another audition that I'd obviously blown, I wanted to party. And just my luck, Sheena's boyfriend, who was an executive for Starbucks was in town and we were all invited to his loft in Manhattan. It was decorated like the inside of a cloud, white and silver. The carpet was thick and soft and bone white and the chandeliers were these strange, lovely things that looked more like sculptures than light fixtures. I was wearing something blue and silky and it was dripping off of me. I sat down on the couch and someone handed me a glass of Pinot and I leaned back, my tan arms looking like some sort of precious metal against the white, Italian leather of the couch. People were laughing, and I recognized an actor who I'd just seen in Woody Allen's latest. I took a snort of coke and sipped at the wine and it felt magical, the music coming from the stereo like a dream. I felt invincible, like I was inside one of the chandeliers, like I was pure light. Like I was pure pure. I began to float. I don't remember falling towards the glass table in front of me, my wine glass smashing against it, my nose gushing blood. I don't remember Sheena calling 911 or the ride in the ambulance to the hospital, where I died, twice. I remember waking up in the hospital, talking to the doctor about all of the drugs, the booze, the late nights. I remember mom flying in from Minneapolis and crying and crying over my bed, my thin, warm white sheets making me feel like a ghost. I couldn't understand it. I was in my early twenties, I was a model, I lived in New York.

Six months later, after mom had taken me home, after months in a room I hadn't seen for years, after a suicide attempt, after counseling, after several hysterical breakdowns on the part of my mom, I was back at Red Stick, at a party at one of Sheena's friend's houses. He was a buckskin actor. He had been bragging all night about the latest Western he had been in, his long black braids glistening in the light, a joint squeezed in-between the fingers of his left hand. My friend Sheena was flirting with crazy Gary Hollywood because she was on shrooms, I was about half a bottle of white wine in, and there was George on the other side of the room, a glass of Patrón in his little hand. He didn't recognize me at first. And then when he did, he smiled. I smiled back. My room in New York had been taken over by another model. She was Jamaican. She was eighteen. I had just turned twenty-five. But some friends of mine had hired me to do PR for a documentary and at least I was out of my mother's house. George came over and told me I looked hot and I snorted and asked him to refill my wine glass. He did. I drank. I thought about all of the stuff mom had been filling my head with for the last six months in between feeding and feeding me, about how I wasn't getting any younger, and did I want a baby, and that my modeling days were behind me, and if I got married how I needed to find an enrolled Native because I was just under half and if I had a kid, that kid wouldn't be enrolled unless I did, and that whoever it was better not be a bum like the people I'd lived with in New York. *Where's Robert?* I asked and it was George's turn to snort. I didn't ask. I drank more wine. And he asked me about my life and told me about his latest film, how it was about Indian boarding schools and I told him that my grandma had been to one and about what had happened to her there and then we ended up in a back bedroom and afterwards, I cried and though he pet my arm awkwardly I could feel how desperately he wished he wasn't there. After about an hour in the dark, my eyes wide open, George got up, and quietly put his clothes on. For a moment I thought he might be pausing to see if my eyes were open or shut but he was only struggling to put on one of his shoes. After I heard the front door close, I got up, and wrapped the long, blue sheet around my body and walked through the now deserted living room and opened the front door. I stood at the door for a while, watching his car disappear down the road, into the desert, into the dark. It smelled like rain and I felt sick and twisted inside like a dark, dark, dying gangrenous thing. I closed the door and walked over to the kitchen and pulled a bottle of tequila out of the mess of bottles. There was blood on the counter where a dancer who George was going to throw me over for at another party in two weeks had taken the cork out of a wine bottle without a corkscrew and had ended up breaking the bottle and cutting her hand deeply. She had laughed and the men had rushed over to help. I went back over to the couch and sat down with the tequila and drank, hard. I lit up a cigarette and tried to push away the deep, wide darkness that was beginning to fill me. I stared at the empty white walls. There was nothing. My God, six months ago, I was in my early twenties, I was a model, I lived in New York.

Gary Hollywood

THE RED GRASSES. That's what I remember. Threading my little brown hands through them on the hills in Oklahoma, my mother calling in Cherokee from the warm little cabin in the distance. The smell of smoking meats. It was so beautiful. But the memory is even more beautiful.

Even then, I knew I was born for blood.

When I drink, I drink for the pain. I drink because I can. Because there is so much blood filling my heart, it's spilling over, I trip on the slick of it. Years ago, years before all of the lights filling my eyes, over and over, the images of me up there for everyone to see, I went to war. We all went to war then, we went because we thought we had to. Warrior warrior warrior, the blood said, but when I left Byron behind in the jungle, I knew what I was.

It was then that I first thought about my dying.

There were times that I thought I could hide in anger, in anger at this country, the things that it had done, the things that it was doing, the people in charge on every reservation, in urban Indian ghettos, in Indian territories. I was so angry it was wonderful. It fed the blood. I remember those days on the Oglala reservation, we were powerful in those dark hills, we were everywhere, like lights, like fireflies, which I've heard are disappearing now, like the bees.

People died there. That fed the blood too.

On the screen, I am terrifying, I am so terrifying that it is utterly beautiful, make no mistake. And I feel like someone should be proud. Look at me up there, my hair so black, my naked chest so brown, my eyes filled with stones. I look like a warrior. I dance, I sing, I fight. I am so beautiful in the dark.

The dark is where I live. God, it's so cold.

When I was a child, my mother would hold me in her long brown arms and rock me in the big wooden rocking chair and sing me to sleep with songs in Cherokee by the little black stove. Dad would come in from work on the ranch and he would smell like big, wild animals and dust, like red red dust. I was half asleep and I could feel her chest rumble as she spoke. Everything was so warm, so beautiful.

Can't I go back? I'm always trying.

I want to say that I've done good things. I have done a lot of good things. I have helped bring our language back. There are things in our words that are not anywhere else in this wide, green world, I know that. There is so much I refuse to leave behind, to lose. I have fought on those red hills. I have fought in the badlands. I have lost things. But there is so much that I lost before I was even born.

The good things sometimes justify the bad.

Sometimes everything is a song, a bird's wing song, *quiet* so you can hear it. I can't hear it anymore, but I used to when I was with her. But she's something I lost too. It hurts too much to think about it, like there's a black hole I was born with, pulling me in.

She had soft blond hair. So soft, like the wing of a bird. I was a child again in her arms.

I hit. I hit. I hit her. I hit her so hard and I hated myself. I can never forgive myself. I left him in the fields. I drink. I push it down.

There is no way back.

When I was in the jungle, I pressed her picture to my heart, my feet rotting in those boots in that deep, black mud and I ran, and shot, I killed so many people, they were everywhere and they were everything they filled up the sky. Byron was ahead of me. He was always leading. He was Ojibwe and he was my best friend. He looked behind to see if I had fallen, because I did once, and that's when the explosions came. They came out of the ground, as if something great and wide had opened up to eat us all. And I ran. I ran. I ran and Byron died.

There is no way back.

On the screen, I feel like I redeem myself, forget myself, I am beautiful. And the women who follow me because of it, giving me beautiful, pure white things to snort and sweet sparkling things to drink understand. When I finally feel like I am underwater and floating and laughing, they all look like her. They never look like Byron. Or my mother. I couldn't live through that.

There is no way back.

Everything is a story, a dream, don't you think? I do. I can see it all from here: the great red plains of Oklahoma, calling me like a song, like a bird's wing, like my mother, calling me in Cherokee. Byron is alive. He lives in Minneapolis. My mother and father are proud of me, and they are still alive. She is still my lover. I live a *life* inside this cocoon of white and sparkling things. I drive around in a shiny, lovely thing, a thing that is like a panther that the women who love me are riding. I just have to keep pushing it all down. Until I crash.

There is no way back.

George Bull

FOR SOME REASON it's the sound of the big, grey van door sliding shut on her face that dusty night in August that I can't get out of my head. Not that I give a fuck. I mean, I was on speed and coke and that little coked up wannabe actress named Brianna that me and Robert had picked up earlier was screaming in Diné and in English about stupid fucking bitches and did I want any more coke. And then I turned off my phone cause you know what, I figured she shouldn't follow me anymore. The dumb broad should just go the fuck home to the stupid house in Albuquerque she shared with that other dancer. It was my fault because no matter how much she pushed me away, I was always coming after her when I came to town. And then I acted like a fucking dick. But it was the industry, not me, and besides, she was always calling me a special Indian, and that pissed me the fuck off.

I'd met the goddamn broad a year back when there was some kind of stupid ceremony the Institute of American Indian Arts was holding. I went because I was gonna try to find this chick I'd met the night before at a party. It was full of Hollywood Indians, most of them poor as shit and sucking at the teat of LA, but one or two with more money than any of us could ever dream at. Her tribe had a fuckton of money and she was someone who could give that money to me so that I could film my latest, which I knew was gonna make everyone cry. It was a pretty short about a Nav chick being taken off to boarding school and the special Indians, as Olivia called them, loved the shit outta that shit. Course my full-length feature about someone accidentally fucking their cousin didn't make anyone cry. Anyone but me that is.

I was also kinda hoping to get laid, or at least drunk. I was hung-over as fuck and tired too but somehow I always found the energy by the end of the day to start it all over again. The damn thing was at the hotel Santa Fe, which was, like every fucking thing in that town, filled with a bunch of pictures of deer and hawks and other Indian shit.

I was texting the hell outta Robert, but he wasn't responding. That was the thing with him. He couldn't party like an animal and get up. I may be a short, fat Nav dude, but I'm an animal. I will take every pill in the room, drink the bottle dry and fuck all night and get up the next day for breakfast with whoever I need to meet with. And it gets me things.

I looked around the room, spotting the cash bar in the corner. Fucking thank God. At half of these shitty things, some self-righteous skin gets it in her head that there shouldn't be alcohol. Fuck that. Though I could see Gary was fucked up already, hovering around the bar and babbling like a newborn. Crazy fucker's played the dude who's gonna hack your neck off in more than half of every Hollywood piece of shit. He was swaying in one of his Miami Vice jackets, spilling bourbon all over the dingy grey-carpeted floor, some big-eyed billyganna broad with ten pounds of shitty turquoise around her skinny neck nodding like mad.

Anyway, there was Olivia in the corner, leaning against the yellow wall, drinking a glass of something that looked like whiskey or bourbon or scotch like some character from *Mad Men* in this bright green dress and I knew I had to get her attention, get her number. I figured she was another goddamn mixed-blood actress, with her long, yellow-brown legs who'd probably try to suck my dick for a part she'd never get because I only cast Navajos, but still.

I was cool. I went over to the table where they were pouring and got myself a shot of Patrón and sat down at one of the banquet tables. I always let people come to me. Olivia was standing around with this goddamn Nav poet, Luis. Could never tell if he was gay but everyone loved him. Fucking poets. He was laughing at something Olivia was saying, this big, genuine laugh and I felt even more anxious to get her number. I looked over at Luis to get his attention and nodded. He looked over at me and nodded back. When I kept looking over he sighed, hard, knowing what I wanted. He waved me over with his short, thin fingers.

I took a long drink of Patrón, the silvery-peppery liquid sliding down my throat, turning me on like a light. I set the crystal glass down on the table and looked around. The room smelled like sage and patchouli, which I hated. I sighed. Drank my glass dry. Went in for another and then headed slowly over to Luis, letting people stop me, kiss my ass. She watched me, looking at Luis curiously. He leaned into her light brown shoulder to whisper something and she raised her lovely black eyebrows, laughed a short laugh. I reminded myself to fucking kill Luis when I had the chance. What was this, goddamn *Dangerous Liaisons* or some shit?

"Hey," I said to Luis. Olivia watched me, sipped at her drink.

"Hey," Luis said in that deep, rich tenor of his. Fucker sounded like a Nav Tom Brokaw.

"How's your girlfriend?" I asked Luis. He hated when people asked about her and I knew it. He narrowed his eyes at me, took a sip at his drink, which was a goddamn pussy ass gin and tonic.

"Good," he said shortly. He turned to Olivia. "Like I was telling you, this is George. He's a filmmaker. A great one."

"Thanks Luis," I said. "But I'm OK," I said, watching Olivia. I didn't want to sound too cocky, though I was already angling for a way to impress her.

"Olivia's a dancer," Luis said.

I remember rolling my eyes. I couldn't help it. There were so many goddamn traditional dancers hanging around I felt like I was wading through a forest of buckskin half the goddamn time.

"Ballet," she said, as if she could read my mind. She looked down at the long, green skirt of her dress and smoothed it. "Though honestly, I'm too old for it, and my tits have always been too big. Good thing I do other kinds of dance, and can teach."

"Olivia," Luis said, laughing and shaking his head. "Dirty."

"Yeah," she said. "I got that mouth in graduate school."

"Sure you did," he said, shaking his head. "I bet your aunties think you're a bad one."

Olivia paused and took a sip of her drink. "I lied. I got my mouth from them." Luis roared and I tried not to but I couldn't help it. It was fucking love.

A FEW HOURS LATER, after a long and ridiculous ceremony, where someone presented a very drunk Gary a flute for some reason I can't even remember, I found myself trapped by this obnoxious Native chick named Lucy. Luis and Olivia had gone for a drink and when I looked up from my phone, there she was, right next to me, panting in my face. I swear to God that broad didn't breathe. And she was at every event, without fail, her loud, ridiculous bullshit about how fucking Indian she was trailing her like a fart. I remember fantasizing briefly about lighting myself on fire. It took what felt like hours to get away from her, as she was yelling a steady stream of ayyyeees and lame powwow jokes at me without taking a breath. Right before she'd come upon me Luis and Olivia had gone for a drink run and spotting Lucy on their way back, took a major U-turn. I could only watch helplessly while they walked out an hour later, Luis looking back at me and whispering into Olivia's ear. Fucker. But I *had* gotten her number and was texting her before she even got out the door. I could see her slip her long hand into the pocket of that bright green dress and look at her phone. She laughed and showed Luis. I winced. I wondered if she would look back. She didn't. I sighed and finished half of my drink in one gulp and started walking towards the bar, Lucy following me. I figured I'd stick around for one more hour and try to work the crowd, see if Gary Hollywood was into any money. See if he was drunk enough to find a way to get some of that money over to me. See if that billyganna with the pounds of turquoise knew anyone who knew anyone who would give me money. The dumb broad I'd been looking for hadn't even showed up. But I was never able to break away to talk to Gary, who stumbled out into the night with his usual entourage, not long after Olivia had, yelling about how the night was young and he was thirsty, the arms and front of his pink blazer spotted with scotch. I looked over at the table where he'd been sitting, where amongst the glasses piled around the table and crumbled white napkins was the flute they'd presented him. I shook my head, laughed and drank the rest of the Patrón.

Lucy had broken away from me when she saw Gary and his entourage leaving and I could see her trailing him and his groupies, most of them already looking coked out of their minds, one thin, blond broad nodding half-heartedly at Lucy as she yelled in her weird Albuquerque almost valley girl accent about some fucking powwow she'd been to recently. Half the reason it had taken me so long to get away from Lucy was because she kept pumping me about where I was going next, watching me watch my phone. I knew we'd probably end up in the same fucking place anyway, but there was no way in hell I was going to make it easy on her.

An hour later, I had just about given up hope on Olivia and was thinking about texting this dumb broad I knew who always answered my texts, no matter how late I texted her. Pretty much *lol* and *where you at?* seemed to be the only things she knew how to type into a phone. But she was there no matter what and gave a great blowjob. Robert had finally gotten up and we were at the Anodyne in downtown Albuquerque, playing pool with this dude Mark Wishewas, a wannabe filmmaker, wannabe writer and overall lame motherfucker, Lucy eyeing me from a booth in the back like an angry Pueblo cat. It was dark and noisy and it smelled like stale beer. Next to Lucy was some Native dude I didn't recognize who looked like he should have a wind machine perpetually centered on his hair. He already seemed like he was ready to chew his own arm off to get away from her, his face angled down permanently at his phone.

I was taking a shot of Patrón that Mark had bought me when my phone vibrated in my jeans. I put the empty shot glass down on the table and pulled my phone out. It was a text from Olivia. I moved away from the pool table and leaned against the wall. I looked up briefly before I texted Olivia back. Robert was talking emphatically at Mark, who was nodding at Robert like he'd just discovered Buddha was in his goddamn midst. Robert had been going on about Oklahoma, about how great it was. One thing I've learned about people from Oklahoma, they love to talk about Oklahoma. Mark, who was also from Oklahoma, was the biggest wannabe kiss-ass I'd ever met. Never did shit on his own. Just attached himself to the next big Indian thing and then talked shit behind their backs. Robert's movie had been taken to Sundance. And so had mine. But his had done better. Much better. Which made me hate him a little. More than a little. Difference between Robert and me is that he *wants* to be a special Indian. He's content to run the circuit. I want out. I only want to make money. Robert had just finished his second feature film and when he wasn't going on about Oklahoma, he was going on about that. Soon it was gonna be about the fucking biscuits his grandmother used to make. If I had to hear about those biscuits, and how normal and simple his life in Oklahoma was one more time, I was going to vomit. I looked down at my phone. Olivia had texted me that she was still in Santa Fe with Luis and some other writers. I texted her back, trying to get her to come to Albuquerque. I wondered why we'd come to Albuquerque. Then I remembered it was because we were staying at the Blue Hotel, which was cheap. I shoved my phone into my jeans and walked up to the bar to order another shot on Mark's dime because I knew I wasn't gonna see her that night and I figured I might as well just get fucked up.

I HAD TO GO BACK UP TO IDAHO for some work for a few months, and I nearly forgot about Olivia. It was good money up in Idaho, and a lot of drugs. I shoot commercials up there every chance I get. And there are no fuckin Indians, which is awesome. But the film festival came around, and my new short was up for an award. They were going to put Robert and me up in style, Hotel Santa Fe, free food, the works. I knew pussy and more drugs were in my immediate future. I got on the plane feeling like royalty, sitting in first class like I was Quentin fucking Tarantino, texting Robert until the second I had to shut my phone off. I waited until the drink cart came by, ordered as many Patróns as I could until they cut me off, then I fell asleep. The only thing I hated about the Film Festival was all the Indians. Hoka Hey this, Aho that, lets burn sage this, this is sacred that. What a bunch of shit. These fucking fuckers wouldn't last two seconds at my parents' house. And I doubt they spoke more than three words of their own language, just enough to pull off looking like a big, important traditional Indian in front of all the people with money. Fuck. But they were treating me good, like I *deserved.*

I was over hanging with Robert and some of his visual artist friends at a gallery where their work was showing. We were drinking wine and champagne and there were a ton of girls and the air smelled good and there were already a ton of parties to get to. And then there was Luis and Olivia in the light of the doorway and the world was even brighter. People were wandering in and out, looking at the art, which all seemed like a blur of deer and long grey hair to me.

They spotted me and walked over, Luis frowning and Olivia smiling that funny, secretive smile of hers. She was wearing a short red dress. Red nails. I smiled back, looked away. Thought about getting another drink. Thought about getting her one. Then thought about how uncool that would look.

"Hey George," Luis said, running his hands through his thick black hair. "Heard you might be here," he said, frowning.

"Yeah, you know, why the fuck not," I said, looking at Olivia and then down at my phone. She was still smiling at me curiously.

"So, you here for the film festival?" I asked Luis.

"Yeah. I was given some money for a short, so, I'm screening it later. You...should come," he said, looking off. I looked over at Olivia.

"You should," she said. "Free booze."

"Sure," I said, trying to sound cool. But I was pissed. Fuckin poet got money for a short, and he isn't even a filmmaker. This stupid business. I figured I would come though, because I wanted to hang with Olivia, and because I wanted to see this shit.

"Where and what time?" I asked.

"6:00 at the Lensic."

"I'll text it to you so you won't forget," Olivia said. "But we have to get going. We're going to meet up with a couple of writers and dancers. And then have an unchoreographed dancing/singing sequence about being between two worlds."

Luis laughed and I couldn't help it, so did I.

"Well, good luck with that," I said.

"Won't be the same without you," Olivia said, her long, slanted eyes painted like an old-fashioned Hollywood actress'. Luis rolled his eyes. I narrowed mine.

They turned and left, Luis whispering something in Olivia's ear as they went, Olivia laughing. God, how I hated that guy. I walked back over to Robert and poured myself another glass of champagne. He lifted his glass, we toasted. I looked back towards the door where Luis and Olivia had exited and drank, long and hard until the glass was empty. And then I poured myself another.

AFTER WATCHING LUIS' SHORT, which was just a bunch of shots of Navajo rugs and landscape with a bunch of color splashed in here and there, I convinced Olivia to come to a party with me. Luis had sighed and looked at her, but she had shrugged and said they should do it. It was a crazy party, Hollywood Indians everywhere, and though I needed to make the rounds, I ended up talking with Olivia the whole night, Luis mostly silent, asking if she was ready to go every time he spoke. She was funny, mean and I wanted to bone her something serious. I tried like hell to get her back to the hotel with me that night, but her goddamn daddy Luis wasn't letting it happen. So I told her that I'd be back in town in a few weeks to work on a collaboration with a friend, and did she have a couch I could crash on. Luis rolled his eyes so hard I thought they were gonna pop outta his giant Nav head but Olivia said sure. She said she had a roommate but that I wouldn't be the first artist to crash on her couch. I just knew I'd make it to her bed by the first night.

TWO WEEKS LATER WE WERE WATCHING MOVIES AT HER PLACE. I asked her if she got high. She said yes. And we smoked out with her roommate until the roommate went to bed. I was sure I was in, but around midnight Olivia handed me a towel and said she had to go to bed. I whined for her to stay up, but she said she had ballet early the next morning. She smiled and told me to sleep well. "Sure," I said. I was bitter as hell. For the next couple of nights I worked on her, showed her my favorite movies, showed her my movie, talked to her like I was her new best friend, but every night she'd go to bed around midnight, every night she left me tossing and turning on their faux-leather couch, the old pink My Little Pony sheets coming off at the edges in the middle of the night.

By the time I left for home, I was frustrated as hell. Hated her a little. And I was out of money and out of work. The shit I'd done with my friend wasn't going to generate any money, and it looked like except for a few stupid Indian gigs, my short wasn't doing that well. This fucking industry.

I went home for a few months, lived with my parents, carried wood, smoked out with my cousins, had a couple of ceremonies and at least got away from the fucking Indians for a while. My phone died, not that it would've worked that well where I was but also, I didn't have the money to pay the bills. And then something broke. It always broke. And I knew I was on my way all the way to the top this time, I was sure of it. Some backers for the feature length I'd been trying to get money for came out of the woodworks, a bunch of crazy fuckers from Dubai. And they wanted to meet up in LA. Were gonna fly me out and treat me like I deserved to be treated. I was excited. And then a little bit of work rolled in from Albuquerque and I knew I was set.

"I DON'T KNOW WHAT I'M GOING TO DO," Olivia was saying. "My gig is about to end at the school, and they're not sure they're going to need me at the studio downtown anymore." We were sitting in her living room and drinking.

"I know that story," I said. I had just told her about my meeting in LA. It had gone well. Turned out some fucking son of a cousin of the King of Dubai had seen the *one* Indian movie that everyone's seen, Barry Four Voice's fucking movie, and loved it. Christ. But it worked in my favor, so what the fuck.

"I thought you had a permanent gig at IA?" I asked.

"No. I just adjunct. But the economy is going bad. And it's always bad in New Mexico. I don't know how long I can stay here." She sighed and took a long drink of the cheap red wine we'd bought at the Liquor store downtown.

"Do you mind if I smoke? I'll open the window." She asked.

"You smoke?"

"Sometimes. When I'm sad."

She lit a camel up and the smell of smoke filled the small house. Her roommate was nowhere to be found. I didn't ask. I'd gone out with Robert that day and we'd been playing pool at the Anodyne when she'd come in, alone. She was drinking in the corner when she saw me and waved. I had motioned for her to come over.

"I'm sick of living like this," she said, her long brown eyes turning on me with too much inside them.

"It's the life of an artist," I said, sighing wearily. I wondered if we were going to have sex, finally, for fuck's sake.

"Yeah, but I'm thirty. I'm a dancer. In many ways, my professional career is over. Yours is just beginning," she tucked her long legs under her and shifted in her yellow dress.

"Well, there are other things," I said.

She frowned and took another puff, tapped her stinky cigarette on her thrift store looking ashtray. It was white with gold edges. It reminded me of my auntie.

"What would those things be?"

"Sex," I said.

"Yes, there is that," she said. She smashed her cigarette out into the ashtray, closed the window, and drank the last of the wine. "There is that," she whispered like a ghost, and came to me.

For all of her annoying sadness, she was funny and good in the sack. So for a few days, I stayed with her and she would go off to work and I would go off to work and then we'd meet up at her place at night. Robert had been texting me every night, asking me to come out, and telling me that I was getting weak. Pussy whipped. I told him at least I was getting pussy, but that excuse was growing old, and besides, she really was annoying with all of her complaining and smoking. I figured I'd get out for good the next day. Hang with Robert. Find some new pussy. Another long-legged mixed-blood actress to suck my dick. One that didn't smoke. Or talk.

"So, I'm gonna head out," I said. She'd come home after me, looking tired. She had immediately sat down on her sagging couch and shook a cigarette out of her pack and lit up. She hadn't even bothered to open the window. She looked up and nodded.

"Yeah. I really should get going," I said, my old blue duffle bag in my hands.

She looked up at me with those eyes that went in too deeply and smiled. "Uh-huh," she said and I felt so much anger. She didn't even seem to care where I was going, who I was going with.

"Really have some work to do."

"Sure."

I sighed, and waved at the smoke, hoping she'd at least crack a window, but she didn't move from her spot on the couch. She was still in her leotard, her legs delicately tucked under her.

I finished packing and zipped my bag up loudly. I headed towards the door and turned around.

"I'll...see you around."

"Sure. Call me."

"You want me to call you?"

She pulled on her cigarette and got up. I thought she was going to come over to me, but she went over to the window and opened it. She sat back down.

"Look, I get it."

"Get what?"

She sighed and lit another cigarette before the other one had even gone out. She pulled at the dying cigarette deeply and then placed it in the ashtray, its smoke curling up and into the room, her new cigarette dangling from her lips.

"You're a party guy, George. You're nobody's boyfriend."

I was silent for a minute. Then, "Well, yeah. Glad you get that."

"But sure, if you want to call me, call me. That would be fun."

"Fun," I echoed. I thought back to a few parties ago. I'd been standing in the corner when this older lady, all done up with huge tits had come over with two drinks in her hands. The brown liquor swirled in the glasses as she swayed drunkenly. She'd shoved one in my face and said, *I've heard about you.* I'd said, *You have?* She'd downed her drink in one long gulp, put the glass down on the table next to her, wobbled back up, belched and pushed her tits into me. *Yeah, I have. Now fuck me.*

Olivia took a drag off of her cigarette. There was only one light on in the living room, and it was grey outside. The light was shining on her neck, and it made it glow in this strange, golden way.

"You know, I loved someone once."

I was silent. I began to walk towards the door. I turned, thought to say something.

"And?" I said, finally.

"And he died on a mountain. He was an idiot. Always doing shit he shouldn't."

I opened the door and left. As I walked towards my car, I promised myself I would never text that crazy fucking broad again.

I WAS HANGING AT THE ANODYNE with Robert when she texted me. I put the phone back in my pocket. I took it out. I texted her back. She came in about fifteen minutes later, drunk. She sat down next to me and Robert. Robert rolled his eyes and looked at his phone. So did I.

"Hey."

"What's up," I said, trying to sound bored and tired.

"Nothing."

I looked down at my phone and she sighed and went up to the bar to get a drink. I watched her.

"When are you going to get rid of her?" Robert asked.

I laughed.

"Really. There are so many other women out there."

I snorted. "It's not like she's the only one I sleep with," I said.

"Whatever man," Robert said. "You're a pussy."

She came back over with a glass of red wine and sat down, tucking her short, pink dress underneath her. She drank from the glass and looked around. Robert and I started talking about his next film, and where he was hoping it would get in. Olivia sighed and looked at the both of us. Finished her glass.

"Well, see you later," she said, getting up. Robert said nothing. I nodded. I watched her make her way through the bar, the white and Indian bodies parting for her as she went. I could see her pull a pack of Camel Lights out of her pocket before she descended the stairs.

A few hours later I was so fucking drunk I thought I was going to pass out in the old leather booth. Robert was gone and I hadn't even realized that he'd left. Relief flooded through me when I finally did realize that he had. I dug my phone out of the pocket of my jeans and texted Olivia. She told me to come over. It was a good thing she lived a few minutes away by foot, because I was beyond too drunk to drive, though I was weaving something serious the whole way, downtown Albuquerque looking like something out of a Dalí. Her house was an old adobe house, with iron bars in place of a screen door. I knocked and a few minutes later, she was there, in a short, baby blue nightgown. She frowned and I came in and tried to sound funny, tried to sound sober, but she just took me by my hand and led me to the bedroom. She pulled my shoes off, my clothes, until finally I was naked as a child. She smoothed my hair. Brought me water. I passed out in her arms. A few hours later I woke up. I looked over and saw that Olivia was still asleep. She was beautiful. I woke her up and led her outside, lay her in the grass, which seemed so soft. It was cold and she seemed afraid. I murmured to her about seeing stars as a kid on the rez, how I missed that. How I loved it back home. How I hated it back home. She nodded and we breathed together and I felt something terrifying there, laying in the grass. Something I couldn't understand. It filled me with emptiness. After we were done, we lay there for a while before we went back inside, looking up at the stars, neither of us talking.

The next morning my head was pounding like a motherfucker, and all I wanted was out. When Olivia stirred, I asked her for painkillers and water. We got up and I told her that I had to get going. She nodded. I showered, put my clothes on. Looked at her. She was sitting on a chair in the corner in the light, smoking.

"See you around," she said.

"Yeah. I mean. I love somebody too," I said.

"What?"

"Well, I went to visit this girl I used to know in Durango. She's Ponca. And you know what...I love her."

"Bye, George," she said, and I opened the door and walked out into the light. It seemed to fill everything up.

I SAW HER ONCE AFTER THAT in Santa Fe, all fucked up. Walking down San Francisco with a couple of friends in the snow at night, laughing, her breath turning to ice. She was wearing these big orange boots and a little wool dress and I remember watching her go, the sound of her echoing off the goddamn adobe buildings until she was gone. I was with Robert and some other guys, so I pretended I hadn't seen her. I was there for some project, I don't even remember what it was. But I saw her in Evangelo's later that night, my goddamn stupid weak heart filling with all of it, and it was on. I couldn't help it. I started chasing her again. And then telling the stupid broad to get lost, all while she blew smoke in my face and laughed. And then I ended up in Idaho again for a long time. And by the time I got back to New Mexico, she was gone. Every time I would get rotten drunk I'd text her. But she never answered. Heard from a couple of people that she'd taken a permanent gig at a University in the Midwest. It doesn't matter. There are so many where she comes from. And it's the industry, I told her that. Now I'm working on a new project and I need money for it but fuck it, I know my break is coming. And she smoked too much anyway, the goddamn stupid broad.

Lucy Bigboca

I'M LUCY BIGBOCA!!! LOL, right? I mean, like everyone doesn't know me already??? Just google me, I tell everyone. LOL!!! I mean, I've represented MY TRIBE in I don't know how many countries, it's ridiculous. And it's a good thing because I'm the ONLY REALLY traditional Navajo in Albuquerque, really the only one!!!

The thing that like, really gets me is all of these Native guys claiming to be traditional when all they are is jerks. I mean, I've dated all of them, like just dated because I'm *sooooooo* traditional? But WHATEV, they're all just afraid of a strong Native woman. Don't they know that I should be the one in charge??? If only they could all be like my cousins, who do what I say, LOL!!!

I mean, and like all of these stupid wannabes, whatever!!! I'm like, LMAO. My dad was a medicine man and my mom is a weaver, OK??? And I'm TOTALLY fluent in Navajo. Just because I don't speak it all the time doesn't mean anything. I'm just, you know, quiet??? I hate it when people like, try to test me with that one, because they're stupid, I'm the traditional one, they shouldn't be doing that, it's not traditional to try to beat a strong Native woman down and if they do it's like L8R!!!

I mean, I went to the Institute of American Indian Arts, which like, has graduated so many famous Indians, and then I even went and got my masters, which is like, extremely rare for Natives. I had to work *soooooooo* hard at it because of all of the other Natives in my program were trying to make me look bad. And my teachers were all jealous of me, I could tell. They were all jealous because I'm *soooo* traditional, and I was like, LMAO!!! Not that it bothered me, it *tooootally* didn't. One of them, who was like, kind of Navajo because she was from the reservation, like tried to correct something I once said and I was like, EXCUSE ME? Don't you know who I am??? I'M LUCY BIGBOCA!!! And she just looked at me AS IF she didn't know what I was talking about. She was *such* a bitch. And she didn't know anything about being a traditional Navajo, that's for sure! She was always talking about how poor she was growing up on the reservation. And like, just because I wasn't poor doesn't mean ANYTHING. I mean, that's a stereotype BTW! Whatev!!!

But really it's all these stupid Native men who think they're so traditional that make my life the hardest. The thing is, no matter how traditional they THINK they are, none of them can ever be as good as my daddy. When my daddy was alive I would go all the time to the Pueblo rez where he was from and we'd do ceremony. And he loved me more than anyone, more than any of his other kids, LOL!!! I'm just sad about the cancer, cancer is such a jerk! It took away the one thing in my life that was like, totally, totally good. I always do the walks to beat cancer, though no way am I going to shave my head, LOL!!! I'm way too traditional, and good looking!

I make traditional foods CONSTANTLY. Yummy! They're soooo good and like, I'm really good at making them, OBV? I mean Navajo frybread's the best! People are like, how do you have the time? And I'm like, I MAKE time because that's what a TRADITIONAL Navajo woman DOES. And my cousins come and they like, help me out and stuff. Though they can be such idiot-babies, I have to tell them what to do the whole way, LMAO! Sometimes if a guy seems like he might not be lame FOR ONCE I invite him to my house and cook with him to show him how traditional I totally obviously am, LOL! And I introduce him to my mom, which is like, serious in my culture? So when they turn out to be jerks, I'm like asshole! I introduced you to my FAMILY, my TRADTIONAL family, and that means something! It means we could be like, engaged.

The biggest jerk of all is this guy named Steven Littlebrush. He thinks he's all that because he's sort of famous in the Indian world and he travels everywhere or whatever. And I'm like, LOL??? I'm famous too??? When we were going out, I even quit my boyfriend, who is really more of a backup than anything because he's SO DUMB. But I like, keep him around, LOL!!! But this guy, he's a painter and he went to IAIA too and he married some stupid white girl and like, had a kid with her or something. But when he was young and like, before all that, we started hanging out and stuff. And he made me feel like he was really traditional, and respectful and honored his culture and respected strong women. He even said that! He said it all the time. We went to powwow together and I met his family too, and his friends were all totally stupid immature guys but at least he introduced me to them and we took a bunch of classes together and he would try to help me with my art, LOL!!! As if I needed it, I was *amazing* at art, I just wanted to like, do more for my tribe and that's why I didn't go any further with it. But I would let him peek over my shoulder at the canvas I was working on and pick out the colors and stuff so that he could feel important. It's TOTALLY important to make a man feel like he has some purpose, though I can barely think of what they're really that good for! I mean, like Native women don't need feminism because for example, I'm the one that's been in control in all of my relationships? So, I don't even need that stuff, that's colonizing anyway. Maybe some of those stupid Native chicks that think they're more traditional than me (as if!!!) could use it LOL!!! I mean, like, most of my friends are guys anyway, because they're so much less jealous. I can't blame women for being jealous of me though, I'm all that! And MEN LOVE ME. I always have a new guy. Whenever the guy I'm seeing turns out to be lame, there's always another. And then of course there's my stupid boyfriend. I mean backup boyfriend, LOL!!!

But I really do deserve a traditional man, and Steven made me feel like for once in my life I was with someone like my *daddy*. Steven seemed different, though all he turned out to be was a big liar. Lame!!! He was with me day and night, painting and singing and dancing and like, really being a cool guy. We were together for a whole year!!! And like, I thought I was gonna marry him, that's how serious we were! My mom loved him and he would sit around in our house in Albuquerque that I grew up in and drink coffee and ask her how to say things in Navajo. And then she'd ask him the words for things in his language but he only knew a few, I mean like, he grew up in some small town in Colorado, so it's not like he grew up traditional like me. Plus he's like, two tribes and like, even though I am too, I'm like, CLEARLY a Navajo woman, like, CLEARLY.

What pisses me off the most is when I think about how Steven played me. Not that I can be played for long, LOL!!! There are too many guys around the corner and I'm smart and educated and hot and just awesome. But he got me to do stuff that like, wasn't traditional? I mean, not like, I mean, I'm not a prude, but I was young. And it's not like I hadn't had boyfriends before, but he made me think, well, he made me think he wanted to have a family. I really believed that stupid asshole! And while I was with him he was just starting to get his reputation and travel and I found out that he was getting it on with everyone! And that's not traditional. And while he was traveling I was texting ILUVU like all the time and he kept texting me back ILUVU and how he missed me. He was probably texting me with one hand and doing you-know-what with the other! JERK! It's like, I'll never trust guys again because of him. And even though he thinks he's so cool now because he's invited to do all of these hip-hop painting performances everyone in the REAL Indian world knows his paintings SUCK! And he clearly barely knows anything about his culture. I know EVERYTHING about being Navajo EVERYTHING.

I'm not the only one that got pregnant with him either. And I remember I didn't even tell him, because I was scared it would push him away. So I you know like, took care of it? And I thought, it's OK, we'll have a baby later, when I'm older and settled and own my own house and am ready. But now that I'm older I've realized it's really traditional to live with your family??? People are like, you're forty and living with your mom? And I'm like WHATEV!!! My mom NEEDS me. And I help out when I can. I mean, it's hard! I need to go out to MAKE IMPORTANT CONNECTIONS and that's expensive. That's not MY FAULT. I got educated. That's what's important, duh!!! At least I didn't get stuck with his baby, especially after I found out he was telling lots of girls that he was their boyfriend. That is SO not TRADITIONAL. There's a girl here that was also going to IAIA and she is stuck with his baby, all while he's with that white woman on the other side of the country!

And I'm TOTALLY planning on learning how to weave too, which I know will make my mom happy and it's TRADITIONAL so I know it's important? But I'm *sooooo* busy, I've got *soooo* much on my calendar, like, all the time. And I know that I'll be traveling EVEN MORE when I start weaving because my mom was famous for her work, and that's why she ended up here, because they wanted her to teach at IAIA, where she met my dad. And so OBV like, that's genetic and I'll be as amazing at that as I am with painting, and with everything else I do. And then Steven will have to realize what he's missing. Which I'm sure he already does!

Sometimes, when I'm high and sitting outside alone on the old plastic deck furniture my parents got when I was a kid, and like, leaning back and looking at the stars I wonder what it would be like with Steven, like, if I'd told him about the baby and if he would have cut it off with all of those other bitches and maybe we could have gotten a place together??? I think about me in the hospital holding a little fuzzy headed baby, Steven by my side. I think about my daddy too, because he was so good to me and how like, when I was with Steven for at least just a little tiny bit of time, I thought that he was almost as good as my dad. And that we were gonna have a life together, a really beautiful life like I had before my daddy died...and then I remember what an ARROGANT JERK Steven was and how he ruined everything and I push that feeling away, because NO ONE is going to bring a TRADITIONAL woman down! That's not how I grew up, that's not who I am!!! I'm a strong Navajo woman! I have to be an example for the younger generation, and like, I already obviously AM.

Robert Two Stories

I MEAN, IT'S MY GRANDMOTHER'S BISCUITS, that's what I miss the most about Oklahoma. That and the people. And of course my daughter. I mean, of course her the most. But the homeless there, the Natives, they were so real. I'd drive by them and think, we could be related. And the hills there, the trees, everything is so green. My life there was so real. So simple. That's what I told the guy interviewing me from *Indian Today*. I mean, it's not like I'm some kind of Cinema Verite guy, like, holding the camera up with my own two hands, I mean, the grant money covered the bigger stuff, but, I do believe in just, you know, letting what you're filming show you what it wants to show you. I was raised to believe in humility. That's what my grandmother taught me. And I really try to bring that into my work. Me and George, we really...try to make the work count. And I've got responsibilities back home. Not everyone has that. But my daughter makes me real. She's very real. Very Oklahoma.

I just feel like the whole Mise-En-Scene of my life is something I bring to my films. The whole mood, you know? I'm just a small town guy, and there was nothing much going on for me growing up. But I loved the movies. They were so real. I remember meeting Quentin Tarantino at Sundance. He was wearing a fuzzy blue bathrobe the whole time and chasing after my friend Charlotte, the Ojib sound tech on George's film. But I could tell he was really interested in me too, told me that he wanted to make it to the screening of my film. And even though he didn't make it, his life is just so Grindhouse, so grainy. I'm sure he had a lot to see. A lot of pressure. I understood. I mean, I totally get it.

Sundance was a lot of fun, though. George and me, we went a little crazy. I mean, both of us are from small towns, we'd never encountered anything like that. So you have to cut us a little slack. We know who we are. That's what's important. Knowing who you are and where you come from. That's what my grandmother taught me and I tried to think of it all as some sort of, you know, like, Reverse Angle Shot, because I was there to promote my work, network. I had to do it. I've always had to prioritize my work even when it was really hard for me. The parties, everything, it was all just to promote my work. What I'm doing is important. And so many people came to my screening, and then after that they gave me more money to make another film and I was asked to screen my film everywhere.

At first, George went with me. He was asked to screen his film too. And we'd screen our films together and party. But after a while he wasn't asked anymore. But I was. He's still asked to screen in Santa Fe here and there and he has his own smaller projects going on, so it really isn't bad for either of us and I know he doesn't really resent me. Not really. What I always told him when this first started happening was that I missed Oklahoma, which he didn't really seem to buy, but I was trying to tell him that he shouldn't be jealous because honestly, I'd rather be at home with my grandmother and daughter. I honestly would.

My grandmother is in her eighties, but she's spry. She takes care of my daughter while I'm gone. Teegan's mother was white. Is white. I mean, I haven't seen her since Teegan was a baby. She just kind of left. I didn't know her well enough, I guess. I did love her though, I think. I mean, she was the first person to really pay any attention to me before I started making movies. We both liked to read and she thought I was really smart. Though really the only stuff I was reading was a bunch of fantasy and comic book shit before I met her. I'd just moved to Tulsa to get away from home. There was going to be a poetry reading at The Gypsy Café where I was working. All I'd ever done in the way of work before coming to Tulsa was bus tables in this shitty diner called Pat's Cafe back home where all they served was weak coffee and greasy eggs and bacon. Just about everyone in that diner was perpetually recovering from a hangover. It was awful to see how many shaking, rough, brown hands there were there, reaching for coffee and looking like pure shit. All I wanted was to get away, to see that time in my life as some sort of Out-Take.

I had been looking forward to the reading all week, and I didn't even have to work that day. It seemed to me like this was a sign that I had really moved into a different place in my life. So when this skinny brown haired girl with big green eyes in a Ting-Tings t-shirt got up and read poems about growing up in a small town in Oklahoma, I just about lost it right there. Talked to her after. She seemed kind of interested in the fact that I was Indian; kind of into it but without being too creepy about it, and after a few hours, we decided that we wanted to go to the bar down the road that she liked. We smoked and drank and talked and I thought that night that maybe through her I would find who I really wanted to be. And we started, you know, kind of dating if that's what you'd call it. She'd come over and we'd listen to music and have sex and she started showing me different kinds of books. Shit. She was the one who got me reading James Welch, my favorite Native writer now. And I told her about how I wanted to make movies. And she told me she thought I could do that. Her name was Sara.

She introduced me to her friends. They were all writers and they all smoked and read their work at the Gypsy Café on Thursdays. She took me to thrift stores, and I told her I'd gone to those all my life, that or got hand-me-downs but she showed me how to really look through everything. Got me these big blocky glasses that looked like they were government issue, but she told me I looked good in them. I remember looking in the mirror in a thrift shop one day in a pea green cardigan she'd gotten me to buy. The mirror was one of those old, weird warped ones with gold marbling all over. She was standing behind me and telling me how cool I looked and I felt like I was going to flood out of my body, back into it and then maybe into hers. And then she leaned forward and into me and I closed my eyes and that's exactly what I did, my body humming with electricity.

Nights, she'd just stand at these big old wooden windows in my place, the brown paint peeling off the frame, her head holding the light, her white feet bare on the wood, the record player we'd bought at a thrift store together blowing something slow and jazzy out. Days, I thought about how bright her hair looked as the sun came up, when she would go for her first cigarette of the morning.

That's when she got pregnant.

When she told me, I'd just gotten home from a long day and all I wanted was to wash the coffee smell off of me and turn on the TV. When I opened the door to the bathroom, she was sitting on the toilet and crying. It took me thirty minutes to get it out of her. When she told me, I was so happy. I figured she was only crying because she figured that I'd be really unhappy about it and she'd stop when I told her that wasn't the case, that I couldn't wait to have a baby with her. But that wasn't it at all. She started shaking and screaming and she threw the tester, the thing sailing out of the bathroom and into the living room. She kept screaming *what about me? What about my life?*

We spent nights arguing, taking turns crying, smoking. I would pull the American Spirits out of her mouth as soon as she lit them, this making her furious, causing her to hit me in the arms, hard.

About two weeks into this, I came home one night out of the blowing snow. The walk had been miserable and work had been non-stop. I had Chinese takeout in my hands, and as I unlocked the door I thought for sure that she would be gone, that she was somewhere getting rid of the baby, having someone cut it out of her. I walked in, my Chucks squeaking on the floor, imagining the horror of it but there she was, sitting on the couch. I stopped and put the takeout down. She smiled. And I knew. She stood up and fell into me and I thought it would be like a Wipe, with the last few weeks moving aside to make room for our new, better lives as parents.

For a few months it *was* OK. Actually, it was kind of beautiful with her pregnant and me in the grocery store buying her things to eat like in the movies, the light of the television at night covering her body like a blanket as she ate the ice cream or peaches or pickles that I'd brought her. And there were her friends coming over and smoking outside and handing us knitted things and my grandmother excited over the phone. And the appointments where they told us that we were having a girl and both of us looking at each other and crying, hoping the baby would have the other's eyes.

And then months later Teegan was born and I felt like I'd never felt before. Important. Like I really finally counted. But that's not how Sara felt. She wouldn't really take care of the baby, wouldn't breastfeed it. Wouldn't get up with it when it cried. I fed it. I got up with it. And after a few weeks she started to disappear, leaving me to wonder where she was all night, the baby crying, me smoking in the dark, haunted and strange. I've never felt so alone or scared in my life. And I knew then one day she'd be really gone, like I was filming her from a truck, a Tracking Shot, her body getting farther and farther away until the fade to black and the Credit Rolls.

When that finally happened and I accepted that it was happening, the apartment so empty, even with her things in it, I decided to go home. Move back in with grandma. She hadn't been back to the apartment in months, and I was behind in rent, in bills, and her cell phone had been disconnected for a long, long time. None of her friends knew where she was. Or at least that's what they told me, though I was never sure.

My dad had never been around much and my mom died when I was really young so I'd been raised by my grandmother. She spoke more Creek than anything, though for some reason it never really took to me. I feel bad about that. That's why I always have it in my movies. English and Creek always seem like they're giving my life a kind of Double Exposure feel, you know?

Once I got home I felt better. Sad and defeated and angry in some ways, but more like I was able to be a dad. I loved Teegan so much. Every time I looked down at her soft long brown eyes and kicking legs as I changed her diaper on the old red couch dad used to sleep on, I was filled with love. I thought that my life beyond that was over, that I'd never do anything important, never make any movies, never leave home. But grandma kept pushing me, telling me she'd take care of Teegan if I wanted to go to college. And it took me a while but I did. I tell you what though, I don't believe in relationships anymore, that's for sure. Women are awful.

They just want to use you. So now I use *them*. I mean, like the man says, "bitches ain't shit but hos and tricks," right? Just kidding. But not really.

I'm just grateful for my grandmother. I mean, she's everything. She's so traditional, and she's raised me right, and now, I mean, when I can't be there, she's raising Teegan right too. Actually, Teegan's learning Creek, which is so cool. I hardly understand the two of them when I get home.

Sometimes Teegan doesn't want to see me and she pushes into grandma's legs when I come through the door, hiding her face. Sometimes she bursts into tears and rushes at me. Kids are weird. Grandma always tells her to cut it out. I don't know why she does that stuff. But when she does, or when I've been away for a long time, I try to Flashframe all of the good times with Teegan in my head, like, when I read her stories by the big black stove in grandma's living room when she was too little to understand, but sat in my lap staring up at me anyway. Or when I picked her up the first time that I'd been away for a while, at college, and she smelled like frybread and violet, that old lady powder that my grandma uses. That always makes me feel better. I mean...I feel bad that I'm not there, but honestly, I'm there a lot. And when I'm not, I'd rather be at home. I mean, it's just that what I'm doing is important. And it might end someday. But I'm sure it won't.

George and I just get crazy when we're together, though the whole industry is crazy really. It's not our faults. I mean, when you're at a party and Tom Cruise shows up and like, everyone's doing coke and you're surrounded by all of these thin, hot white chicks drunk as shit, I mean...I always feel like my head is the camera, and we've like, decided on a really shallow Depth of Field and everything around me is out of focus except for what's right in front of me. And I just try to have another drink, and another, because otherwise I just don't think I could handle it.

And then there are the Indian parties. In Santa Fe mostly, but sometimes in Minneapolis or Denver when there's a big Indian film festival or we're screening for a Native audience. Honestly, those are more fun. George hates them. Calls them the sage burning, hoka heyyyy crowd. But we're treated like fucking royalty at those. Tall, yellow-brown, beautiful Indian women the kind I never grew up with are everywhere, and we're treated like everything we do is special, sacred, like what we're doing will never end. The only part that sucks is that all of those chicks are either looking for you to cast them or they're done with being a model/actress and they're searching for a Native husband. And like I said, I'm not into that. I've got enough responsibility in my life, and I've already got a kid. And that's what these chicks want, an accomplished Native dude who they can have accomplished Native babies with, and man, they think I've got what they want, but I don't. The funniest thing is when they're like that with George. I mean, he makes it totally clear that he's in it for the coke and to get laid but these women will just go wild over him. After a few days, the shit completely hits the fan. Because he has no problem with getting all over one chick the first night we're there and a totally different one the next. And those chicks like nothing more than to compare notes. Luckily, we're usually out of there before there's blood. Though one time these two chicks George boned were at a party together and they were like, best friends or something or at least they acted that way. Then one of them points to George. And that crazy bastard, he's busy hitting on number three. He doesn't even notice the impending cloud of feminine doom gathering above his head. Pretty soon both of them, one of who was our ride there, are yelling at him, their pointy maroon nails getting all too close to his eyes. Both of them were practically twice as tall as him too. He's just shrugging and saying nothing but I'm on the phone, calling a cab. Nothing gets to that guy. He doesn't care about any of them. He's like a freaking machine. There was this one girl though...a ballet dancer. I didn't like her, because she thought she was so funny and smart and George just wouldn't quit running after her. It really irritated me. I mean, we're a team, that's the way it is. Bros before hos, right? Not to sound sexist or anything.

Women give birth. That's hard. So I respect them for that. And like I said, it's my grandmother who really saved me. My dad was a giant douche. I hated it when he'd come around, all drunk and stupid. We'd have to listen to him go on and on about shit I didn't care about, the government, his drunk friends and their stupid antics, pounding Bud after Bud until he passed out on the couch, the stink of him moving through the whole house until he'd wake up sometime the next day, shower, eat and disappear again, the back of his greasy Metallica t-shirt the last thing I'd see of him. What really used to piss me off the most was when he'd go on and on with advice for me, about women or life. I have this Montage in my head. It's me, sitting on grandma's old grey couch opposite to the old red couch he used to like to sit on when he'd come over: me at five nodding, me at twelve nodding, me at seventeen nodding, always silent. One time I woke up and came out into the living room. Grandma wasn't up and I remember going over to the couch and staring down at him. The unmistakable smell of urine was radiating off of him in waves. I remember looking down at him. I think I was like, thirteen or something. All I could feel was pure hatred. I just wanted him to disappear. He didn't even move.

George isn't like that. He's the hardest worker I know. And he sticks by me, pretty much no matter what. And he's fluent in Navajo. I never heard my dad speak one word of Creek. He didn't even want to. Grandma talked about what a rebellious kid he was, how much he wanted out. How much he hated being Creek. Hated Oklahoma. I don't get that. I love Oklahoma. It's my home. George says he loves it back home too. We really understand each other, or at least that's how I feel. I feel like I am Oklahoma, that it's the only place where I'm real. And George, he's real close to his parents, his family, his whole community. Shit, his dad's a medicine man. And I respect the hell out of that. It's just so real. It's like when we're together, it's a Two-Shot, walking, talking, partying, helping each other with our movies.

One of the best times George and I had together, if it hadn't been for that stupid ballet dancer getting in the way, was this one night in Santa Fe. I was showing my new film and he was debuting his new short. We were staying at the Hotel Santa Fe and they had set us up with everything we might need and there were Indians who loved film flooding the streets. I remember eating at Geronimo where we'd had dinner with Gary Hollywood and Robert Redford and a bunch of Hollywood Indians from every buckskin flick I'd ever seen and thinking that this was a dream. That this was not real. After, we walked out into the streets of Santa Fe, and it was dusty, and lovely and the whole night was alive with the sounds of bars and restaurants serving beautiful Mexican food and the adobe buildings and the church were glowing in the desert as the sun went down. George was walking next to me, a circle of beautiful Hollywood Indians surrounding him, laughing at his dirty jokes, and he just looked at me and I knew he was thinking the same thing and he pulled a little baggy of mushrooms out of the pocket of his jeans and I took one even though I never did shit like that and then soon, it really was a dream. The whole night was, it was floating out in front of me, the colors of the night like a Klimt, shimmering and gold. Everyone was laughing and I felt as good – no better – than I ever had with Teegan's mom.

I even remember feeling OK about my dad, that he had had it hard and that I had to understand that. That he was just the way he was. I looked over at George in that waking dream, and saw my dad smiling at me, a Bud in his hand, his favorite Metallica t-shirt on his skinny little back and I laughed. And he laughed back, his fat little stomach rolling out in front of him like a ball bouncing. And then it was George laughing and yet it was still my father and that didn't bother me at all. I felt a blazing fire on my right and I turned and there was a Virgin de Guadalupe in the window of a shop. The light was overwhelming. I put my hand over my eyes to shade them and walked over to the window and it was lit up like daytime in the desert, this big metal sculpture with my grandmother's face at the center of all of these metal flames that were blowing in a soundless desert wind. My eyes started to adjust and grandmother smiled and I felt this beautiful feeling, this electricity in my heart, in my whole body and I went down on my knees and she put her hand on my head and I prayed in Creek, though I don't know how.

I don't even remember getting to the Cowboy but suddenly I was there, underground, looking at the crowd like I was a Wide Angle Lens, everything was coming to me at once. Then it was as if there was some sort of Cross Cut, because I didn't remember going to another bar but suddenly we were somewhere else and George was talking to these three coked up Nav chicks. And across the room, leaning against the long wooden bar, was the ballet dancer. She was with her little poet friend, this guy who me and George hated, and I prayed George wouldn't spot her but he did. He waved her over and one of the three chicks who was really already nuts over George and the most coked up of all of them eyed her like a snake. In fact she turned into a snake, a big black one and I remember backing away from her, bumping into someone and spilling my drink. The snake hissed at me and I shuddered.

All I remember next was the snake yelling at the dancer and the dancer telling her calmly, "fuck you." Then we were outside and two chicks and a snake were shoving George into a van. A few minutes later the dancer came out of the bar. I realized that she was my only ride if I wanted to get back to George because I had no idea where my wallet was. She asked me if I wanted a ride. I said yes, George texting me the whole time, half indicating that he didn't want her there and half indicating that he did. But when she tried to call him, of course he wouldn't pick up. She lit a cigarette and I asked for one and we rolled the windows down enough to let the smoke out. She told me that he'd chased her down the night before and begged her to come up. Otherwise, she didn't have a place to stay. I resisted the urge to feel sorry for her.

Once we got to the hotel it was more booze and more drugs and the three chicks saying pissy things to the dancer and the dancer rolling her eyes, sitting cross-legged in the corner of the room in the old Southwestern style hotel chair and sipping her gin and tonic like she was in a fucking Bond movie. I was really coming down by that time from the shrooms but with the help of some coke I felt good again, like partying all night. The dancer was clearly tired of the whole thing, not even taking any of the coke and slowly sipping on her one gin and tonic for what seemed like hours. Finally around 4AM I took two of the chicks my room to fuck and left George with his dancer, the third one stumbling to her room down the hallway, looking less like a snake at this point and more like a lost and wounded puppy in her shiny black heels. She was the one who would have been George's if the dancer hadn't tracked him down. I'd thought about taking her too but she seemed too fucked up to do anything.

The next morning I felt like dying and so I sent the two chicks back to their room so that I could be sick alone. I spent the day getting sick and sleeping and watching TV, and when George started texting around six to come out, I texted him that there was no fucking way that was going to happen and went back to sleep.

The film festival ended with the usual bang and whimper and George posted a bunch of arty pics of the chicks we screwed on the internet and then got in trouble with a girl he'd told he loved in Durango, some Ponca chick who he'd met a year ago screening his film there at the college. After the festival ended, I went off to another university to screen my new film.

I keep asking people how they like it because it seems like, I dunno, like they like the first film more and like, well, the general response is kind of different. I even asked the dancer about the film on the way to the hotel because even though she's a stupid bitch, she does have a Masters and everything and I figured her opinion sort of mattered. I remember she was kind of quiet for a while, smoking her Marlboro thoughtfully and then saying, *I thought it was fairly well done.* Whatever that means. What does she know anyway, she's a fucking ballerina.

I know George is a little pissed about the fact that I got money for another full length feature film and I know we're not spending as much time together lately, but...we're still friends. It's just that I'm always busy. It's not my fault I'm getting work. The weirdest thing though is that ever since that stupid ballet dancer left town, he's gotten all buddy-buddy with that loser Mark Wishewas, the wannabe filmmaker who also dated that stupid dancer. I don't get it. All he did was complain about him and now they're filming something together. It's like some Double Exposure nightmare.

The thing that really pissed me off though, I mean, not like it's that big of deal but like, when my dad died, it's like he didn't even give a shit. I mean, I don't give a shit either, like I said my dad was a jerk. But when I got the call, we were at some party in LA at some crazy producer's house. It was one of those hilariously just like in the movies white mansion deals with a giant pool that looked like it came with chicks in bikinis in it. We were having fun, drinking expensive multicolored drinks and talking with a ton of producers and actors and directors and I was freaking out because I recognized so many people. And of course George was swimming in women.

About two hours in I could feel my cell vibrating in my pocket. I was tempted to ignore it. It was still early in the evening and things were getting wild and beautiful and I was feeling that feeling of just, I don't know, glory. But I had felt a little tug at my heart when the phone had first started vibrating. When I pulled it out, I could see it was my grandma, who never called. I excused myself and walked into one of the empty rooms in the back and sat down on the bed and felt strange and sick. And then grandma told me he was dead. That he had died by drowning in his own puke in an alley. And I felt so angry and ashamed and I told her I'd be home the next day and hung up.

I walked back into the party, changed, feeling deflated and sick and like the punch had just gone out of things. George was still surrounded by women, and they were laughing and he had his hand on one of their long, tan thighs. The white lights that were strung up everywhere that had looked so lovely and mysterious a few hours ago now looked ghostly and they filled me with a kind of unnamable feeling, almost nausea. I told George that we had to go. He ignored me for a bit and then looked at me impatiently, irritation crumpling his little purple lips. He just kept saying for me to wait, to chill out, that he was having fun. And I kept saying that it was important, that I really had to go. He just kept brushing me off like a douche and finally I was forced to yell that my dad had just died from choking on his own vomit outside of a bar in Tulsa and could we please go? And the girls around him got silent. And then George rolled his eyes. Just a little. Just for a second. But I saw it. He handed me the keys to the rental car and told me that he'd get a ride home. I ripped them from his small hand and walked out of the party, people yelling and laughing and drinking all around me, feeling sick and confused and angry and hating those people, just hating them.

The valet drove the car around and I got in and drove off, the weird, dry smell of California coming at me in the night, and I wondered what the fuck it all meant. Trying to look at it all like it was from a Long Lens, like it was already beyond me, and I was sitting at home with Teegan and grandma and it was years past the time when we had to bury my dad, years past the time that George acted like fucking a random chick was more important than being a friend, years past me having to go to any more of these parties, years and years and years from now.

Mark Wishewar

I KNOW I'M SMART. And a great filmmaker. Just because I haven't filmed anything doesn't *mean* anything. I know what I'd film would be ten, no, *one-hundred times* better than what those other Indians have done. They don't even *deserve* all the attention they've gotten. I mean, I'm going to be working with George Bull, and though he acts like he can barely stand me, I know he thinks I'm a genius.

If I could just get rid of Laura. She's always *on* me, and it's really annoying. I never should have hooked up with her in the first place. That was a total mistake. And I know I keep having sex with her, but it's just because I'm so used to her by now. She's so young; it makes it easy. That one time I hooked up with that crazy bitch Lucy and Laura started screaming and crying outside the door cause she'd followed us home from the bar was just awful. It's just that I hate confrontation and besides, every time I start something with a new girl she ends up being one of those Indians who gets everything and it just really bothers me.

I went to the Anondyne a few weeks ago to get a drink and just you know, relax, see if I might run into anyone I know and there's George and Robert Two Stories playing pool, looking deep in discussion. I figure that they won't mind if I join. So I walk up to Robert and like, kind of stand behind him and George but they don't see me and keep on talking. That's the thing with these guys, they're *so* self-important. It's amazing how big and important they think they are, like the whole stupid world is listening. The hilarious part about it is that no one outside of the Indian world even *cares*. The only Native filmmaker they give a fuck about is Barry Four Voices, and he's really a writer anyway. And he's someone who's gotten more than he deserves too.

Anyway, finally I just start tapping George's shoulder and he like, sighs like I'm fucking five-years-old or something and then turns around and smiles at me from below. Because you know, he's like, barely over five feet tall. I tell him *hey* and ask if I could I buy him and Robert a round and they look at each other and shrug. I smile and go up to the bar to get drinks all the time thinking about how I'm going to go back there after I get their drinks, slam the drinks down on the table and tell them that I think they're overrated nobodies.

I stand at the long, wooden bar fuming, trying not to face punch the drunk white guy next to me who keeps elbowing my ribs when the bartender *finally* pays attention to me. I get myself a beer and order shots of Patrón cause that's the only thing George will drink. He thinks he's some kind of Navajo *G* I guess. I walk back over to them, my heart pounding in my chest the whole way, and hand them their tequila. They don't even thank me and continue playing. I stand near them, my arms crossed over my chest, wondering if I should just retreat to one of the sticky, red, duct taped booths and drink a few beers on my own. I feel like I'm being turned inside out listening to them talk on and on about George's latest. It's something about the whole boarding school thing, which I'm so tired of I could puke. I mean, Jesus, what about talking about how we are now? That's what I was always thinking about when I was thinking about writing a short story collection though I never had time to write it. I mean, I work in a library and that takes up a lot of my time. Plus the writing world is completely full of crap. I'm totally done with it. At least film has an audience. Plus, the writers I meet are always total jerks.

Finally I tap George on the shoulder and he sighs again like I'm stopping him from building the Mayan pyramids and turns around and looks at me, not even opening his mouth to speak. I feel like taking that pool stick that's in his short, stubby brown hand and cracking it over his head.

"Mind if I play?" I ask and he looks over his shoulder at Robert, with his stupid wannabe Johnny Depp stubble and hipster glasses.

Robert shrugs, says, "Sure. We were just talking about you, Wish," and hands me his pool cue. I start to sweat because *what the fuck did he mean by talking about me* but I take the pool cue and George sets up the balls and takes a shot without even asking me if I'd like to take a crack at them, which I'm actually really good at. I ask him about his new film, and though at first he barely acknowledges my presence, after a while, after I buy him and Robert, who's hitting on some new Indian chick I've never seen before more shots, he starts to loosen up. He goes on and on about how everyone loves his film, not that he cares. He talks about all of the old Native chicks who cry introducing it and laughs and asks me for another shot after he wins the game, which I go and get for him, nervous the whole time wondering if he's going to replace me while I'm up at the bar. I keep looking back but he's just joined Robert and they seem to be competing over the new girl, who's tossing her long dark hair behind her ears and laughing, never talking. I frown. It's bullshit how they get all of the women and leave nothing for the rest of us. I mean, when's it my turn?

I get the shots finally and walk back over to them, having to nearly push people out of my way it's so crowded and hand them their drinks, which they take. The girl squeals, "What about me?" And she laughs flirtatiously but not really at me. "Yeah, Wish, what about Gillian?" I want to tell them to buy drinks for pussy themselves but I laugh and go and get her a drink. When I get back and hand it to her, assuming that she wanted Patrón, she looks at it and asks, "What's this?" George says, "Patrón baby, you'll love it." She scruntches her nose like a five-year-old who's just smelled a dog fart and demands a long island ice tea. "Snap to it, Wish," George says and Robert laughs. I feel like killing them both and take the shot myself, and walk back up to the bar. This will all pay off, I know it.

I come back with the Long Island and the stupid girl practically jerks it from my hand and starts sucking at it, not even looking at me. I sit down next to George and try to strike up a conversation again about doing a project together. That's the thing about George, he's always got his hands in some kind of money, he's always hustling.

That's not me. I'm an idea man. Last time we talked, he seemed interested in what I was saying, about doing something about Oklahoma. I mean, George does stuff about the Navajo Rez but he's always saying that he doesn't want to do that anymore, that he just wants to make money. So I figure I can kind of use him as he's on his way up. He's got a lot of connections, and I've got a lot of great ideas, so I think we'd make a great team. I mean, I emailed one of the writers that are getting so much attention who is at least writing about what Indians are like now in Oklahoma and he said that he'd work with me but I just need...you know...the connections and money first. *That's* why I didn't email him back. I'm sure I would write better stories anyway. And I'll get something together as soon as I can get George to help me. I mean, really I'd be helping *him*. His films aren't that good but he just keeps *getting* everything, so I've just got to take advantage of that.

I kept eyeballing George and trying to interject, but eventually George and Robert just went off with the chick, mumbling something about getting high in George's hotel room. They didn't say anything about me coming, but I wouldn't have wanted to anyway. I'm really not into parties and I like to go to bed early. I mean, I have a job. A *real* job that I had to go to school for.

I walked home feeling pissed, telling myself that I was paranoid and that George would text me for sure the next day to talk about our project. When I got home, I pulled my phone out of my pocket. I could see that Laura had called or texted like, fifty times. I sighed heavily. She was *so* annoying. I texted her to come over.

About a week or two after that though, I got shit figured *out*. All of the great ones just crashed into shit, knew they were entitled to it, right? That's what George and Robert do. I had had this whole thing wrong the whole time. What an idiot. I mean, not like I'm really an idiot, just like, I'm an idiot for not getting it sooner. All I had to do was get my ticket to the Red Stick festival. Nobody's going to believe how famous I am in a few years. All I have to do now is wait for it to come to me.

HONESTLY, I WAS PRETTY BALLER. The first day of Red Stick I texted George and Robert. But this time, I didn't care if they texted back *at all*. And since they're spoiled shits, they didn't. Normally this would have really pissed me off. I would have sat in Evangelo's all day and drank cheap beer after cheap beer, watching all of the stupid pseudo-famous skins walk through the door, yell stupid Indian jokes at each other, and leave to have stupid, pseudo-famous Indian sex. But I didn't. I went to a screening of a film *all on my own* and sat through the whole thing. It was a documentary about basketball on reservations. It was all about how it's actually really traditional to play basketball and empowering and stuff. About these two teenage girls that everyone's wild about because they've won a couple of games. I fucking *hate* basketball.

After the film, I saw this girl I kind of knew. I'd taken a summer class with her at the Institute of American Indian Arts and I could see her talking to the director of the film. I walked up and said hi and even though she looked like she didn't recognize me at all, I started talking to her a mile a minute so she couldn't get out of talking to me. See how I'm really starting to figure it all out? The director was this obnoxious looking guy with ridiculously long hair and a huge, insanely expensive turquoise necklace that looked like he'd bought it yesterday somewhere in downtown Santa Fe on the plaza. I walked right up to him and introduced myself. He looked kind of annoyed because he'd been talking to some people, but then when I said I was a director he looked like maybe I might be someone important and paid attention to me. He asked me what film of mine was screening and I mumbled something so that he couldn't really understand me and then I asked him where the after party was. See, you have to be a go-getter. And I was tired of waiting my turn. That's not what Robert and George do. No way. They *take* what they need. He looked at me funny and then said that he was going to probably have dinner with friends and then go to bed. I elbowed him and said, "Sure, but what about the VIPs?" He looked at me for a moment and then said, "I'll tell you what, you give me your number and I'll text you if anything is happening later. I promise." I felt a surge of excitement and whipped my phone out and told him that I'd call his number so he'd have it, but he said, "That's OK, why don't I just put your number in my phone?" So I gave it to him and we talked for a bit more and then I walked over to the girl I knew, whose name I couldn't remember. She had a funny expression on her face and I was sure it was because she was impressed. I asked her if she was going to dinner but she just sighed and turned away from me.

I walked over to Evangelo's to celebrate. I had a green chili cheeseburger and fries and then sat at the bar, staring at my phone. I talked with a couple of guys at the bar, told them I was there for Red Stick. A lot of them were there for it too, mainly minor actors. Man, those guys kill me. There was this one dude I met, skinny as hell, hair dyed jet black, Native guy from Vancouver. Drank nothing but gin and tonics, one after another. But he never seemed to get drunk. He was living in Los Angeles off of this broad. "She hot?" I asked. He shrugged. He was dressed completely in black, black tank, jeans, all black like some kind of throwback heavy metal rock star from the 80's. The only thing on him that wasn't black was his belt buckle, which was in the shape of a gun, and made of diamonds. "Your woman give that to you?" He shrugged. Told me that he did a bunch of buckskin parts where he was always killed off. Said it was work, at least he was playing Indians. He left. I looked at my phone. Had another beer. Talked to another buckskin actor. By the time the bar closed, all I'd gotten was a text from Laura asking *What's up?* Of course I ignored it. I wasn't gonna let her get in my way.

On the way home, I thought about the girl from IA and the director and how maybe they and like, Robert Redford were all at the Cowgirl eating and drinking and having a big laugh at my expense. Then I realized how ridiculous that thought was. I mean, being a director is exhausting, that's what George says. He's always talking about how that's why he needs to wind down at the end of the day with some drinks and drugs and chicks. That makes sense. Though I don't know if I could handle all that drinking and drugs. Maybe just the chicks.

Anyway, I crawled into bed that night feeling pretty good, pretty proud of myself. I looked at my phone and there was another text from Laura. It said *lol, u better b careful or ill go home w someone else.* I rolled my eyes and turned off my phone and pulled the covers up. I was in a Motel 6 on the edge of town. I had gotten a hotel because I'd known that I'd need to be in Santa Fe for Red Stick. I was sure that the next day was going to be even better. I was going to go to the best screening I could find and tell Robert and George so that they could see how I wasn't taking shit anymore.

The next day I was sitting in the theatre, watching a stupid film about Inuits. I remembered seeing the director's name in the paper a few months back. The film went on forever, and I could barely understand it but I decided that I was definitely going to make something happen this time. After the film, I went up and started talking to the director. He was definitely impressed. I mean, I've read just about every book by every Native or Inuit writer ever. So I know what I'm talking about. He told me that a group of them were going to have dinner that night and that I should join them. I told him that I'd have to check my schedule but that I thought I could manage. "This festival is madness," I said suavely and he laughed and nodded. "The hangers-on are what drive me the craziest," he said and I laughed nervously and pushed for his phone number.

I went to town for some lunch, and sat down and immediately started texting Robert and George to gloat. *Good for you, Wish,* Robert texted back about thirty minutes later. I laughed and ate my burger. I knew he was jealous. It was obvious. They were gonna wish they'd treated me better. They would be begging to work with me someday. I wish that Robert *would* work with me. His film did really well at Sundance, unlike George's. Plus, we're both from Oklahoma and Robert is always talking about how important Oklahoma is to him. Me too. It's *so* important to me. I mean, I don't want to go back there but it's still the most important thing in my life.

That night, at the Blue Corn Café I told the chick at the front that I was meeting a group. "I'm a *director,*" I said, leaning in. She just looked at me and then said I was free to look around, but that as far as she knew, no one was looking for a Mark Wishewas. I looked all around the restaurant but that director whose name I couldn't remember wasn't there. I walked up to the bar and sat down on one of the tall, wooden chairs and ordered a Corona. I traced the metallic countertop with my finger. I walked back over to the chick at the front and told her that I was happy to start the table. She looked at me for a few seconds, her buggy green eyes practically popping out of her head and then asked how many people were in my party. I said I didn't know. She sighed and told me that since they were really busy, that she couldn't seat me and an invisible party of people, especially if I didn't even know how many were coming. I felt a surge of rage and told her that I was a *director* and that there were other *directors* coming, *"Really important guys,"* and that she should watch out because they could have her job. "I'll get my manager,"she said.

I leaned against the wall and waited, looking at my phone to see if the director had texted. After a couple of minutes, she came back with the manager, who asked if we could sit at the bar together and talk. I explained the situation and he nodded and said, "I tell you what. You have another drink on the house and the minute your party comes in, I'll personally see to it that you get a table." I told him that would be satisfactory. He nodded, shook my hand and signaled for the bartender. I ordered another Corona. I looked at my phone. It was 6:3o, a half hour after he said he'd come. But he was a *director*, he was *important*. And plus, he was an Indian director or at least you know, an Inuit one, so he was sure to be late as hell. Not me. I had never been one of those on Indian time guys. I'm always early.

A half an hour later I was sure I'd been ditched and was ready to shove a burrito into my face and then go to Evangelo's and drink. This was bullshit. I mean, I had really *done* something. And I deserved for it to be my turn. I was thinking that as soon as I remembered that director's name I was gonna go tell everyone about what a douche he was and he'd never work again. But in the middle of my working myself up into a frenzy, in comes the director, a group of Hollywood Indians right behind. I got up real cool and slow and walked over to him. "Hey," I said. He narrowed his eyes thoughtfully and didn't answer and I could tell he didn't know who I was, at all. I felt sick. Then he broke into a smile. "It's that guy I was telling you about!" he said, clapping me on the arm. I just about shit I felt so good. I walked over to the stupid chick up at the front and she sighed and got us menus and led us to a table. I impressed everyone with my knowledge. I really do read a ton. And there was one girl at the table, this blue-eyed Inuit chick who was just gorgeous and she was eyeing me in this *really* obvious way and I was so glad that soon I could just ditch Laura, that my life would be *filled* with women like this.

After dinner everyone was pretty drunk and in a really good mood and no one wanted to end the party so I suggested we go to this bar that I went to *all* the time with Robert and George. Well, at least, I usually saw them there and then hung out with them, which is pretty much the same thing. I was sure they'd be there, which would be awesome because then I could rub it in their stupid faces that I was with really important people, like I'd been texting.

Walking down the street we were loud, and the streets were loud with directors and it seemed like everyone was drunk, and everyone was important. I was even sure at one point that I saw Winona Ryder. Supposedly, she loves Indians. I wondered for a moment if I would become so famous that Winona Ryder would want to have sex with me. I shook my head and laughed at myself, but in the back of my mind I knew that if this day was any indication of the future, that could happen.

We walked down the steep steps into The Underground. It was wild with music, the deep, damp, smell of beer rising up to meet us as we descended. I waded through an ocean of dark hair, Robert and George appearing nearly the minute I started to make my way to the bar. I nodded at them and though they acted like they barely noticed me, I was sure they were jealous. I figured I'd be big about it all and buy them some drinks. Hell, why not, they were soon going to be begging *me* for attention. And they were always poor.

After telling the crew that I had some people I had to talk with, I walked up to the bar and bought a round of Patrón and started to bring the drinks over to Robert and George and stopped. There was that goddamn Indian ballet dancer I'd almost hooked up with a while back. She was having some sort of argument with another girl and Robert and George were just standing there looking stupid. I could hear George say something like, "Cool it girls," and the ballet dancer walked off. I went over to them and said, "Glad she didn't see me," and nodded towards the dancer. "Why's that, Wish?" George said, sounding testy. He was watching her go. "She's crazy. I'm sure if she'd have seen me I wouldn't have been able to get away from her," I said. And George just took both shots of Patrón from my hands and gulped them down, one after another. "But that other one is for..." I said, and Robert clapped me on the back, the silver bracelet around his wrist making it sting. "It's OK Wish," he said, pulling me away from George, which made me feel anxious. I looked at the dancer. She was at the bar with that crazy Pueblo bitch Lucy, who was talking at the dancer like her mouth was some kind of machine gun, the dancer nodding and obviously looking around for a chance to escape. I hoped she would stay over there. I could see the girl who'd been arguing with the dancer yelling at George, who was nodding and sipping at a drink that had seemed to appear in his hands spontaneously after Robert had pulled me away. The girl was really young. And she looked totally fucked up. But she was hot. She looked sort of like my Laura. Navajo for sure. Then she was gesturing wildly at George who was staring blankly at her, and then over at the dancer. She started pulling George towards the exit and he had to violently push her hands off of him. I thought this would make her mad, and she'd storm off but instead she started stroking his chubby brown arm. Then she laughed and walked off towards the bar presumably to get another drink. Robert sighed and followed her.

"Why are the hot ones always crazy?" I said, walking back over to George and standing next to him. That seemed to be the right thing to say, because George laughed and then said, "You're alright, Wish." He asked me what I was doing there and I told him about all of the great stuff and George nodded and looked at me like I was important. I looked back, my heart beating hard. I knew this was it. I took a deep breath. "We should do something together," I said. "You know I've got great ideas." George looked at me, his little brown eyes full of some kind of emotion I just couldn't get at and then he said, "Sure, let's talk about that." It was then that I knew all of my hard work was going to pay off. That there would be a point where I'd go home and my family wouldn't laugh at me for being a piddling librarian. No one would ever laugh at me again. I was about to ask George about when we should get together when the crazy Nav chick came back. I thought she was going to hand him yet another drink, but she started pulling on him again and this time, he let her drag him out, smiling at me as he went, a couple of chicks on the stairs yelling, "Come on!" I turned around to look for Robert, but he was over by the dancer, who was nodding as he talked. She was looking over at the exit and running her hands through her long, dark brown hair. They talked for a little bit longer and then left together. But that was OK. I looked around for the crew I came in with, but they were nowhere to be seen. Even Lucy was gone. The only person I recognized was this crazy actress who'd gotten fat and was always hanging all over George. She was staring at the crowd, her eyes like the inside of an abandoned truck. I walked over to the bar and leaned in, working to get the bartender's attention. I waved at her and she looked annoyed. I smiled. She put her back to me, reaching for a bottle of something violently green. I began to tear up, my throat constricting. A few minutes later, the bartender came over and I started to order a beer and stopped. I smiled again at the bartender who didn't smile back and said, "I'll have a shot of Patrón." I watched her go, her short shorts riding up, the hot, wooden smell of the bar so familiar and cruel.

Olivia James

ADAGIO, ADAGIO, ADAGIO, slowly my arms pull across the blue New Mexican sky. I'm so careful with my arabesque, it's so long and slow, adagio, adagio, adagio, this is dangerous. We bourrée across the stage towards the finish, all of us like a wave of tall, ocean plants, our roots undone, skittering across the bottom of the sea. As we finish, and the crowd stands and applauds, I keep my balance, and then we bow. I love it here, but there are too many ghosts. But then again, there are ghosts everywhere.

HE PASSED ME THE BOTTLE OF CHAMPAGNE and I drank, the pink stuff I insisted on, the good stuff, pouring down the sides of my mouth, even though I'd tried to make sure that wouldn't happen. To him, I'm just another thin, beautiful, ubiquitous dancer. Maria Tall Chief, he called me. When he asked me if I was Italian, I had laughed.

"Come here," he said, and I scooted closer towards him in the back of the long white limo. We were on our way to a party, and it was moving down the streets quickly, the lights from the street reflecting eerily inside the limo as we passed the street lamps, like we were on the surface of Mars. I looked up. I'd always wanted to visit Mars.

I leaned against David, his tongue on my neck. "So much trash in New York," I said.

"You love the trash," David said and I ran my long, thin fingers through his thick grey hair. I could feel his excitement as I did.

"Sure I do," I said.

"You love me," he said.

"Sure I do," I said.

He sighed. "Olivia, Olivia, my tough little Indian."

"I'm 5'10. I'm hardly little," I said, rolling my eyes. He couldn't see them. He was kissing my neck. I let him go on for a while before I asked the question I'd been burning to ask since we left the auditorium. "Was I good tonight?"

"There was no one more beautiful."

"But was I good."

"The best," he said, but I couldn't see his eyes.

I REMEMBERED GOING TO POWWOW AS A CHILD. Daddy had started me dancing when I was two at the Indian Center downtown. When I started as a Tiny Tot, first at Fancy Shawl, then at Jingle, I won often. Won at Denver March. At Gathering of Nations. But I didn't care. I had begged my father for ballet lessons since I'd first seen it on TV, the women swimming across the screen, so beautiful I thought my heart would burst. Those women could do anything, go anywhere, they were magical, they were magic. I lived in a shitty apartment on Colfax in Denver with my dad. He worked at the Presbyterian hospital as a janitor. But he found the money for lessons, because I wanted it. And daddy was so sweet, he always gave me what I wanted.

The only thing I loved more than ballet was our Saturday mornings. Daddy would wake me with coffee and cereal, whichever kind I wanted. From the time I could remember, I insisted on something that would keep me thin. We would talk about our dreams. He would ask me about school. And he would always try to get me to eat more, because I would never finish the bowl. I knew even then that this life was all about discipline, about denial. *But you're already tiny!* Dad would say and I would frown. *Don't do that. You break daddy's heart.* Then I would feel like crying. Daddy had it hard. Mom left when I was young, and he didn't talk much about her, except that they had met when they were children in Oklahoma, that she was Choctaw and white, that she had been beautiful and tall and mean and funny. I knew that he still loved her, still thought she might come back. I knew she wouldn't. I couldn't even remember her. Maybe sometimes something would smell like her, like sweet almond oil, but I thought that's what I wanted her to smell like. And I knew all of daddy's dreams were about her.

IN NEW YORK, I WAS IN LOVE. *Développé, the teacher yelled, and our legs arced out and bent and moved slowly, painfully outwards like fans unfolding. En dehors, he yelled, and the circle began, and it hurt. I loved that pain. I was hungry. Not for food, for this life, this dance, these lilies after the show, for the stiff, pink tulle of our skirts, for my teacher's love, approval, I couldn't tell the difference. He was much harder on me than on any of the others, and to teach him that I was no one he could mess with, I would stay after, and do everything again and again until the lights would go off. Then I would ride the subway home to Brooklyn, my feet pounding, to another shitty apartment in another city that I shared with other dancers and artists, and I would fall into bed so that I could go to work the next morning at the coffee shop around the corner, so that I could live here, so that I could stay inside the magic for as long as this life would let me.*

IT WAS WHEN I WAS SIX that I began to take ballet. There was a little Asian girl in the class, the only other one that didn't look like a little blonde angel in a leotard that had obviously been recovered from the local thrift store by her daddy, and I gravitated towards her. But she frowned and moved away and right then and there I determined that I didn't need any friends, especially any girls as friends. The teacher had eyed me and my father curiously in that studio in the middle of Denver when we came in, my father looking shy and huge and so incredibly brown next to all of the thin, white mothers in their expensive running suits that even then, I suspected they never ran in. I was reminded of that scene in Alice in Wonderland, the one where Alice is picked apart by all of the nasty lady-flowers. But I stood tall as my father told me he would come for me as soon as the class was over. He had offered to watch me, but I had told him that that would only make me nervous.

We began with the simple stuff, the baby stuff. But I had been doing traditional dance since I could remember, and I could move. The movements were different, but it was still dance. My tiny body bent and pointed, swayed, shuddered to the music. I loved the long, shiny wooden floors, the sound of the teacher's voice, sharp and direct and forgiving when it could be, because after all, we were still children. I didn't feel like a child. I felt like a soldier. A beautiful determined soldier with her hair up in a tight, angry, near-black bun. By the end of the class, I was tearing up. When we applauded, the tears escaped and I ran up to the teacher and hugged her thin, bony, hard-with-muscle body and her arms came over me and when I finally moved away, I tried to look as if I wasn't crying. But there at the door was my father, and there were tears in his eyes, and the teacher smiled that thin, teasing smile that so many dancers have and I knew I had come home, home, finally all the way home.

"**TELL ME YOU LOVE ME**," *David said.*

"Of course I do," I said, rolling over in bed for a cigarette. We hadn't had sex for a week, and David was beginning to be in a mood about it. I kept telling him that I had to save all of my energy for our upcoming performance, but that was a lie. The truth was that I knew that David was the kind of man you had to keep wanting.

"But you never say it," he said, sounding mopey and weak.

I lit my cigarette and breathed in, the smoke jetting out into the cold, white-carpeted room, decorated in what David referred to as tribal. I supposed I fit right in. I looked down at my thin, yellow body, hard with muscle. I was strong.

I tapped the ashes into the crystal ashtray by the side of the bed and asked David if he wanted one.

"Yes," he answered and I handed him the pack.

"I thought you were quitting," I said, drawing my legs up.

"I'm European. I have to smoke. And watch futbal. Or they revoke my citizenship."

"When was the last time you went home?" I asked, looking at a large, red painting of a woman that David said had been a gift from someone long ago. She was tall and ethereal and there

was something distant about her. It was my favorite painting in the apartment.

David was silent for a moment. "Three years ago. For my mother's funeral."

It was my turn for silence. Then, "I didn't realize your mom was dead."

There are a lot of things we don't know about each other," he said and took a drag.

"YOU'RE NEVER GOING TO LEAVE YOUR DADDY, are you?" Dad asked, and I squirmed. I was twelve, and practicing barre while watching a video of *Swan Lake*. Dad had found some materials for a makeshift barre at the junkyard outside of town and had nailed it all up on the side of the living room wall. He had even taken our carpet out and put wood floors in, another find from the junkyard. The video and the VHS had been acquired from the thrift store we liked to browse through on Saturday afternoons. I liked those afternoons, looking through junk, through all the racks and racks of dusty-smelling clothes. I was good at finding things that looked nice on me and daddy was good at finding things he could fix up. The TV had been given to us by one of the guys daddy played cards with on Friday nights. Occasionally, white lines would run through the screen, but it wasn't that bad. And my teacher, who I loved dearly, gave me all of her videotapes to watch and practice with. I had started pointe the year before, and I was getting so good that my teacher was already talking New York, talking professional. She even let me come into the studios on Sunday when she wasn't busy. We would run through routines, and she would correct me, shape my body, my mind. It was all I thought about. She had looked at me one Sunday, her lean body taut in the small wooden chair she was sitting in, her left hand massaging a sore foot. She stopped massaging and laughed, watching me practice a soubresaut. "You love this too much. It will be the death of you, you know."

Dad was sitting at the kitchen table, a cup of coffee in his big, rough brown hand, *The Denver Post* in the other. "Of course not dad. But I have to grow up," I said, my left hand on the barre, my right leg executing a round de jambe. It was one of my favorite actions at the barre. They were so elegant and precise. All neatly tied up, the leg strict and straight and elegantly curving into a half-circle on the floor.

"No, I don't want that either."

I stopped dancing and looked over at him. "You're silly dad."

He looked over at me and said something in Chickasaw that I didn't understand. He would try to teach me a few words, and I remembered some, but all of the Natives around me were Navajo, or Lakota, or some Oklahoma mix like me, so what I knew in Indian was a mash-up. I understood more Spanish than anything in Chickasaw.

I smiled at him, and he looked sad then, like I'd already grown up and left, like I was already far away. I went over and hugged him, hard and he held me, stroked my hair. Then he got up to make some more coffee. He stood at the window while it brewed, staring out at the grey, snow-covered streets, the light falling, the shadows on his face like a dream.

"DAVID, WHEN ARE WE GOING TO EUROPE? *I want to do just one show. I love New York. It's wonderful. But I want more. I want Paris. I haven't come this far only to stop here. I know that the best dancers stay here, with the New York City Ballet and it's not like I want to tour, I just want to dance in Paris, just once."*

David sighed and put his fork down. We were dining in one of his favorite restaurants, a French restaurant. He knew the owners. Somehow there was a connection that led back to Europe before he'd come to New York. We were eating oysters, which I loved.

"You have your audition," he said, a slight smile playing on his lips. "Why do you think I ordered champagne?"
I squealed, and I realized that I hadn't felt like this since the time my daddy had taken me home to Texas for my birthday. Almost all of his relatives had settled in Dallas, and he'd saved up his money, and we'd driven for hours in his blue, beat-up Chevy until we were in front of my auntie's little house. I had been surrounded by family. This was like that. It was better.

"I'm so happy!" I said, and reached over and squeezed David's hand.

"I have requested some time off from the school and you will be in-between shows, so we can tour Europe." He looked at me, love and affection clear in his gaze. "I can't wait to see Europe through my little Indian's eyes."

My head was filled with images of Paris, the Eiffel Tower, shoe and clothes shopping for the latest in Parisian fashion, parties in glamorous, golden-lit restaurants, streets filled with stylish and expensive-smelling people.

"But you will have to work hard at that audition. New York is now Paris, and Paris knows it."

I laughed, and the champagne came.

"We both know that's the one thing I can do," I said, watching as the waiter poured. I kept my eyes on the champagne. David hated it when I tried to engage anyone waiting on us, though I generally rebelled and did it anyway. But tonight was special.

David picked up his glass, and I mine, and he held his out. We clinked, and drank. "We both know you are good at many things. One of them working hard, the other...at holding the hearts of men."

I laughed again.

I HAD THE SUNDAY OFF ONE WINTERY, New York day, and so I had decided to go into the studio to practice. I had taken the subway into Manhattan with my big pink dance bag by my side, my tights and leotard underneath my large, woolen thrift-store jacket and gotten off at the stop I always got off at, pausing for a coffee in a local shop. I had told the teacher that I liked to practice on my own, and that I would like an extra set of keys. When he had responded to my request with silence, I had taken that to mean that he didn't trust me. I was filled with rage but had said nothing. But after the next class ended, he had handed me a set of keys with a strange, knowing kind of smile. I thanked him airily and walked immediately out the door, sighing with relief when I felt I was out of sight.

My coffee in hand, I walked down the streets of New York, happy to be there, happy to be living somewhere other than Denver.

New York was somewhere no one knew me, the sheer mass of people shuffling past making me feel a kind of lovely, gentle melancholy. At the studio doors, I dug for the keys I'd so coveted in my bag, found them and unlocked the doors. Inside, I turned the lights on and listened to them hum. I set my bag down, threw my coat off and tossed it into the corner and then sat on the hard, wooden floor so that I could put my silky pink pointe shoes on. I shoved my boots off and began to get into my pointe shoes, thanking the Creator for the new gel inserts. The old wooden toe and cotton stuffing had been a form of torture. I stretched for a good twenty minutes and then began the newest routine. I knew each step by heart. But I wanted everything to be perfect. To be elegant, magical. I turned the music on. I began to glissade. And then I started into the rest of the routine. But what I needed to make perfect was my fouetté rond de jambe en tournant. I had been working on that for a long time.

I had practiced the routine over and over, for several hours, had broken for a small lunch I'd packed and then continued, focusing on my fouetté rond de jambe en tournant. I had done it successfully fairly quickly, but I wasn't satisfied. I began to curse over the music. I paused, leaned against the barre and then started again. Until I was half-way through another turn, and cursing a loud blue streak into the air, I didn't notice that the teacher had come in at some point in the last few minutes and was watching me in the doorway, his arms crossed over his chest, a teasing smile on his lips. I felt a shock pull through me and then decided to ignore him. I started again, this time without cursing. He watched me practice, and I was filled with an icy rage that made me want to hit him, to scream at him as loudly as I could, to be better than any dancer he had ever trained. I went through the full routine again, determined not to let him stop me. He had been particularly cruel this week, coming over again and again, hitting my legs with his stick, yelling in that quiet way of his that made me want to kick that stick out of his hand and hit him in the face with it. One day in bed, I realized that he'd hit me so hard with the stick there were bruises on my calves.

This time, my turn, my fouetté rond de jambe en tournant was perfect. I could feel it before I even began, it was everything it was supposed to be. I began to tear up, but I kept going, finished the routine. I wanted to yell, "HA!" in his stupid, white, billyganna face but instead I stopped, ready to gather my things and leave without a word. I began to stride over towards my bag.

"Stop," he said.

I looked over at him, my long black eyes like a cat's. He smiled at me. Said nothing. Just as I was about to continue walking, he came over to me. He slid his arms over mine.

"Like this," he said, directing me, his breath hot on my neck.

"David..." I said, my rage becoming something else.

"**ARE ALL INDIAN WOMEN LIKE THIS?**" *David asked.*

"Like what. I'm me. I'm only me," I said. I hated when David got like this. Petulant. Angry. But a quiet angry. We had just had a wonderful dinner, I had killed at my audition at the Opéra de Paris. David had been pleased, and as I finished, I could hear whispering up front. La belle amérindienne, c'est magnifque! And of course, tout comme Maria Tall Chief, tout comme!

"So dominant. So like a man."

We were sitting at a table. We had come to a restaurant his friends had wanted to go to, to celebrate. David had many friends. Many ex-lovers who were now friends. And I had taken French in high school, and had taken a refresher course in New York. His friends had expected a silent American, a stupid girl. They were surprised when I spoke French decently, they were surprised that I was funny, that I was dark.

I had always been quick. And quick with language, because when you grow up with so many languages around you that you must learn, or get pushed down into the dirt, you learn fast. I had never been pushed down, around. I had had too many men around me, admirers, boys who I knew exactly how to keep close, but not too close. This had begun when I was five.

We were alone. His friends had left us to celebrate our last drink on our own. One of them had left an intricately carved white plaster mask. I put it over my face. "You must like fucking men then," I said.

David was silent. I thought for a moment that I had finally pushed him too far. I put the mask down and stared at him placidly.

I wondered what he would do. Would he slap me? Cry? It was exciting. He began to laugh. "I love you so much Maria Tall Chief. You will be the death of me."

I put the mask down and took a long sip of my champagne. "It will be your best death ever."

David smiled and gestured for the check. "I can't wait."

IN NEW MEXICO, there were so many Indian boys. I played with them all. What was left? I was nearing thirty, and there was no more Paris, no more professional ballet, no more David. And the other boy...I had to push that down. Far down. As far as it would go, or it would drive me to madness. There were times when I was mad. When I would drink and drink and cry in the apartment I shared with the other dancer. She was sweet, but stupid. When she would see me do this, she would pet my head and tell me how sorry she was. That her heart had been broken too. I would nod, and thank her and not tell her the precise way it had been broken. I *was* like a man, David was right. I always kept my pain deep inside. Except for the tears. I guess they made me a woman after all.

"THERE WAS SOMEONE ELSE," *David said, his hand in mine.*

I looked down at him. I was taller than he was by two inches, and I wore heels. He didn't mind. In fact, he loved them. He always came home with a new pair. We were walking down the Rue de Passy at night, the reds and blues and whites of the store fronts lit up beautifully, the shops looking like something out of dream. They were. I had dreamt of them. I had dreamt of all of this.

"There is always someone before someone," I said. I dropped his hand and walked over to the front of the store, staring in at the tall white mannequins in clothes so fine, so glamorous it hurt my teeth to look at them.

"Yes," he said, standing next to me and staring into the window. I could see our reflection, David, his soft grey hair in a sophisticated cut, his casual but expensive clothing nearly shining in the light above us. I cocked my head, examined my long, thin form, my dark hair sweeping over my shoulders and down my back. "But there is...

more. *There is someone important. I can feel him there, when we're
making love. I don't like it."*

"Aren't we beautiful?" I said, looking at our reflection.

*David sighed, picked up my cold hand. "Yes. We are very
beautiful. Especially you. You are like a butterfly. A cold blue
butterfly."*

"But when will I fly away?"

"Daddy, tell me you're proud of me."

It was graduation, and I had a scholarship to a school in New
York, the very best school one could go to if one wanted to dance
professionally. And I knew after that it was a short trip to the New
York City Ballet. We were sitting in the Denver Diner. We were
there to celebrate.

Daddy looked up at me, his eyes sad and soft. I felt a twist in my
belly and in my heart that I could almost not bear. I began to cry.

"Don't cry sweetie. Of course daddy's proud of you," he said
putting one of his fries down and patting my hand awkwardly.

"I think you should move to New York with me," I said.

Dad looked at me with such intensity, and then laughed, his
head shaking at the end of it. "I love you too," he said.

"Really daddy, why not? You could get a job at a hospital there.
There are loads and loads of hospitals in a city like New York. And
that way I wouldn't have to be lonely," I said anxiously, knowing
that he would never take me up on it, wanting him to, not wanting
him to.

"Oh, sweetie...sometimes a person has to feel lonely. And
don't you worry about your daddy. I like my job, and my friends.
I have a life here. And you need to have a life too. A different life,
God willing."

I nodded. We ate in silence for a while, me picking at my salad,
daddy finishing up his roast beef sandwich and fries, the smell of
fried everything filling the air. I thought about a different life. I
had always wanted out, knew I didn't want to be a thing like the
people I went to school with, all babies and drugs. I remembered
once I'd spent the night at a girl's house. We had become friends in

AP English. I liked her. She wore huge, government issue glasses and read all the time. Her mom was raising her alone and was gone most nights. She worked at the hospital too, night shift. We'd spent the evening studying and talking about what we were going to do after high school when we'd heard a knock at the door. I remember Sabrina sighing heavily.

"That's probably my cousin. She's always knocking on my door when she's drunk, when her stupid boyfriend has beat the hell out of her and she wants some sympathy." Sabrina pushed her large, blocky black glasses further up her nose and got up. I followed her into the living room of her sagging apartment. She walked over to the door, her body heavy, and opened it. Sabrina's cousin marched in, a tiny blonde girl of no more than fifteen. Her hair was huge. More hairspray than I thought a single can could contain had gone into the elaborate construction of what she was wearing on top of her head. It was like her hair was a separate entity.

"Yeah, let's get drunk," Tina said, pulling up a gigantic bottle of vodka and swigging from it. "I wanna celebrate."

"Tina..." Sabrina said, but she marched determinedly towards Sabrina's bedroom, Sabrina trailing behind.

Tina plopped down on Sabrina's bed, pushing her Biology book off the bed in one careless swoop. "Good times," she said, swigging again.

She looked over at me. "Who's the Mexican?"

I rolled my eyes.

"She's not a Mexican."

"Well, she is kinda light. Eye-talian then."

Sabrina took the bottle of vodka out of Tina's hands, or should I say, tried to take the bottle, as Tina clung to that thing like it was magical potion.

"She's an Indian, if you must know," Sabrina said, walking away from the bed and leaning against her white and gold dresser. She glared at Tina.

Tina looked over at me with some interest. "Really? Me too. I got some Cherokee in me. You Cherokee?"

"No."

"Well, then what kinda Indian are you? There aren't that many, you know. Least around here. Lots of Mexicans though."

"Chickasaw. And Choctaw." I hated this girl.

"Well, never heard of that," Tina said. She stared at me, her blue eyes rimmed in layers and layers of black eyeliner.

"So...why the celebration?" Sabrina asked.

"Not pregnant. Not anymore, anyway."

I looked over at Sabrina, who shrugged.

"What do you mean anymore? You get an abortion? Man, hope your mom doesn't find out. Isn't she born again Christian?"

Tina took a long, hard gulp of the vodka and then paused. I wondered if she was going to puke all over Sabrina's pretty white bedspread. Sabrina had told me that she'd saved up for months from her bussing job for that bed. Had put it on layaway at Sears.

"Fuck that bitch. Bitch had loads of abortions before she became *born again*," Tina said.

"Then..." Tina said.

"Oh. I just got Ralph to hit me in the stomach, over and over, hard as he could, till it came out."

I felt sick. I looked over at Sabrina whose face quickly contorted from one of horror to nonchalance.

"It's great, right?" Tina said, not looking at either of us. She just took yet another long swig of vodka and then offered it up to Sabrina, who shook her head. She looked over at me. "Well, I won't ask you if you want any. On account of you being Indian and all. You know you guys don't do well with the ol' firewater."

"Thanks," I said, walking over to stand near Sabrina.

"Sure. I just don't want you getting all outta control or anything."

"Right."

I looked over at Sabrina, who knew that after her cousin's revelation, there was no way in Christ she could tell her to leave. We spent the rest of the night listening to Tina alternately cuss and then praise her horrific sounding boyfriend until she passed out, her legs splayed in two very awkward positions, her right hand still desperately clutching the handle of the bottle of vodka.

"DAVID, DO YOU REGRET NOT HAVING CHILDREN?"

We were sitting outside in Rome. We'd had a good day, walking around the city, looking at all of the ruins, drinking wine and eating at a little restaurant that David had been to many times with one of his exes. He loved the prosciutto.

David took a sip of his wine. He looked at me. "Do you want a baby?"

I looked back over at him. "Of course not."

"You are only nineteen. There is plenty of time for that, for babies, when all of this is over."

I felt a sharp pain then. I signaled for the waiter. He came over. "Hi. Un altro?" I said, pointing to my glass.

David looked at me, sipped again. The light was fading and it was beautiful, the walls of the outside of the restaurant were covered in ivy, and the little tables were all covered in crisp white cloth, everyone speaking Italian in soft, clipped tones.

"You are worried about when this is all over," he said. When the waiter returned, he pointed to his glass as well.

I sat back. David could be so dense. "Of course I am."

"You should not. Because first of all, you have many years until that comes. And you need to learn to enjoy life."

"I do—"

"Wait," he said, interrupting me. "Let me finish. You need to learn to live in the moment for once. You are always looking ahead, looking for more." The waiter returned with his wine and he sipped at it before he began again. "All artists are like this. It is necessary, this...disposition you have. Otherwise you would have been satisfied with your life as it came to you. You would never be here, in Rome, about to perform. But there comes a point where this is damaging. Do you want to end up like Edith Piaf?"

I began to laugh, hard, at the thought that I'd end up a love-struck heroin addict.

David frowned. "You laugh now, but you don't know what it's like to live your whole life as an artist. So much has come to you so very young. And you have demons, just as she did."

I crossed my arms across my chest. "I'm listening."

"Secondly, when that times comes, you can open a studio. And you could even open one in New York, which is a wonderful city. Your life as an artist will not be over."

I picked at my salad. "That's...not. Yes, David. You're right. You're so good to me," I said, patting his hand.

David looked happy, satisfied, like we'd had an argument and he'd won. I stared at a family at the next table, the mom reaching over and feeding her little, fat baby and smiling at him. He smiled back at her, his mouth covered in food. They seemed very happy, the baby and his mother.

I WAS AT A PARTY WHEN IT HAPPENED. My friend Shaun had been bugging me to go during lunch that day. I always sat at the jock's table, because there weren't many girls. And because there were ways that I had much more in common with them than with anyone else at that school; I was praying my body would get me out of this. I told him that I never went to parties. I told him they were boring, because they were always full of boys, which made the boys around me stir anxiously. I remember hitting Shaun in the chest gently, and the light that came into his big amber-colored eyes when I did it, the envy and violence that came into the eyes of all the boys around him. I laughed happily. I left the lunch table with Shaun and his friend begging me to come.

That night, studying in my little room, I thought about Shaun's invitation. I was sure it would be a waste of my time, loads of drunken kids gathered around a stereo trying to have sex with each other. I looked up at my posters of Maria Tall Chief and Yvonne Chouteau on my walls. I would stare up at them often, into them, knowing that if they had done it, I could. I was staring up at them that night like they were other galaxies, full of wonder and mystery and life. I was feeling restless. I walked over to my dresser, where I'd casually tossed the piece of paper Shaun had pressed into my hand. I picked it up, looked at his juvenile scrawl. It had the address of the party on it. It was two blocks away.

At the doorway to the house, I could see the lights of the house glowing brightly, the noise of the party nearly stopping me at the door. But there was something friendly and warm and vaguely exciting about it all, and I knocked. There was no answer. I knocked again, and then opened the door. The noise was deafening. I began backing out, pulling the door closed when a boy I knew from school saw me and rushed over. "Olivia! Don't go," he said, pulling at my arm. I smiled and followed him in.

"You came! You never come!" His name was Jamie and he was a friend of Shaun's. I let him take me by my hand and pull. He shut the old, wooden door behind me. "Let me get you a drink. You like beer? Or something, uh, classier? Like vodka? Let me get you some vodka!" I smiled and began following behind him. As we rounded the corner towards the kitchen, I could see that the house was packed with people, drunk, loud people, all screaming over the music at each other, some of them dancing, some of them sitting on old, patterned couches in the corner of the house. I hesitated, and he turned around and smiled and pulled gently, and I let him lead me into the kitchen. He was a football player, and my hand was swallowed by his meaty palm, my arm looking like a long, muscular stick extending out from his, though he wasn't much taller than I was.

In the kitchen, we were surrounded by people. My high school was big, so it wasn't any surprise that I didn't recognize anyone. But I felt awkward since I never went to parties. I was quiet, thin, had a way with boys, and only talked to jocks. If anyone did recognize me, I can't imagine they would want to socialize. And what would I say if they did? When the boys would talk about their dreams after high school, about their injuries, about how hard their coaches were on them, I could relate. But except for the occasional female friend, like Sabrina, my concerns were hardly the same as the average high school student. I smiled as Jamie handed me a plastic cup full of vodka and sipped delicately from it.

"Good, right?" I nodded and sipped again.

"So, where are you going for college?" I asked. I knew Jamie wanted to play college football, had already been given a couple of really good offers, scholarships.

"I'm thinking University of Iowa," he said, drinking half a can of Bud in one gulp.

"Yeah?"

"Yeah, they're gonna give me a full ride. I mean, and I'm not that bad at school. I'm not one of those jerks who expect to slide. I mean, I'm not like a rocket scientist or anything, and believe me, if I get to play pro I will, but I know this could be it. I plan to take full advantage. I'm gonna major in business, and start my own if the pro thing doesn't happen," he said. He looked at me like a satisfied puppy.

"That's a great plan," I said.

"What about you?"

"Well...I'm just going to try to get into the best dance school I can in New York and go from there," I said, sipping more vodka and looking around. A girl ran into the kitchen yelling and laughing, a boy behind her. They both stopped at the keg and pumped beers for each other, the boy slapping her ass in mid-pump. She squealed in mock rage.

"Hey, wanna meet some of my friends? We've met through various games and other sporting events over the years. Not all of them are football players. A couple basketball players, some runners, you know."

"Sounds dangerous," I said and Jamie laughed.

The music grew louder as we left the kitchen and entered the living room, the smell and noise of young, wild humans filling the air. Jamie walked over to one of the couches, threading his way with his enormous bulk through the crowd. There was a group of boys sitting on the couch, and they seemed to be happy, laughing and talking easily.

"Hey," Jamie said, "This is Olivia."

"Hi," I said and they all nodded and a few reached up to shake my hand.

"So, you...play basketball?" One of them asked me. He was a tall, lanky guy who looked like he definitely played basketball.

"No. Actually, ballet. I mean, I don't *play* ballet, I perform it," I said, regretting the way that had come out of my mouth.

"Oh. Well. You look sorta like a basketball player," he said, "tall and strong."

"I could definitely wrestle you if I had to," I said, sipping my vodka. They all laughed. I liked to say flirtatious things.

The boys began talking about the last basketball game they'd watched together and I began to drift. This is where what I had in common with jocks faded. I was more into my French class, into reading the books my friend Sabrina recommended. Though I did like watching sports, as long as no one asked me to engage too thoroughly. I sipped at my vodka for a bit, thinking about the homework I should be doing, about how upset my daddy would be if he knew where I was when I realized that I was being watched. I came out of my reverie and looked down at the couch, where a tall, smaller-framed boy was sitting, his legs crossed, his gaze directed up at my face. I blinked.

"Hello," he said, I'm Tomás."

"Olivia."

"So I've heard."

I looked down at him. He seemed very arrogant. I didn't like arrogant men. They were much harder to control. I looked away and into the party, wondering how I would duck out. What excuses I could make that wouldn't upset Jaime.

"Have you seen Shaun?" I asked Jaime, tapping on his massive shoulder.

"Oh, yeah, he was here. But he left about an hour ago with that chick…Oh, shit, whatsername? She's a cheerleader. Red hair."

"Ah," I said. It would be easy for me to go. I sipped a little more on the vodka. "Nuthin' but a 'G' Thang," started thumping through the air. I liked hip-hop, but I wasn't very good at it. You had to be strong in a different way. I was about to tell Jaime that I was getting tired, that I had ballet the next day when I was interrupted by Tomás.

"So, dancers are strong?"

I looked down at him. I felt irritated. He smiled.

"Yes."

"But you're so skinny."

"But I'm very, very strong. And besides, that's the way it works in ballet," I said impatiently, turning back to Jaime, who was high-fiving one of his friends and laughing.

"I know it does."

I looked back down at Tomás, my irritation growing.

"You know what does?"

"That it works that way in ballet," he said, leaning further back into the couch as if he was sitting by the fireside in an extremely expensive restaurant. He was a good looking guy, his rich black hair curling ever so slightly.

"Then why did you ask me?"

"To get a little rise out of a dancer."

My eyes narrowed. "What is your problem?"

He smiled. "Sit by me."

I was incredulous. "Why on God's green earth would I do that? So you can spend more time getting a *rise* out of me?"

He laughed. "Yes. Plus, my mother was a dancer. Ballet."

"Well, doesn't someone have mommy issues," I said, thinking this would surely piss him off.

"Oh, definitely. I have mommy issues you can't imagine. Let me tell you all about them," he said, patting the couch.

I sighed with exasperation and turned to Jaime, who was still occupied with his buddies. He was describing a pass with great animation.

"Give me a chance," Tomás said. "You won't regret it."

"I already regret it."

"You're sharp. I like you," he said, drinking out of his red cup. "Sit down and I'll get you another of whatever you're drinking."

"No. I have to go. I have practice tomorrow, and I never come to these things anyway."

"Me either, but I thought, why not? I'm graduating. And you're only young once."

"You're a very strange boy," I said.

"Yes. I am. Now let me get you a drink. Let me redeem myself. I can't help teasing you. You're clearly so used to getting your way."

I turned to leave and he stood up and touched me on the arm. I looked back like an angry cat, ready to pounce.

"Can't you take a challenge?" he asked.

"Certainly, though I think you're not trying to challenge me, but piss me off. What I can't figure out is *why*."

"Maybe because I like you."

I laughed. "You hardly know me. And I'm not a very easy person to know. Or a very nice one, once you do get to know me."

"I doubt that very much."

I turned to Jaime. "Hey Jamie," I said, tapping insistently on his arm, "I've got to go. Ballet tomorrow."

Jaime looked sad. But he understood.

"Goodbye, Tomás," I said curtly.

Tomás shrugged and sat down.

As I walked out, I thought about Tomás, about boys like him. Why were they so determined to reach inside and grab at something only because it was unknown to them? It was as if they simply couldn't stand it when someone didn't just roll over and start whimpering whenever they were around. I opened the front door and I couldn't help it, I looked back. I could see the couch from the door and there he was, staring back at me. I narrowed my eyes, turned around, and walked out, glad to be rid of him.

A few days later, I was sitting on my bed, watching the sun go down and listening to *Clair De Lune*. I was dreaming of Paris, of women in ethereal white skirts moving across a stage, when the phone rang.

"It's for you!" dad yelled from the living room. I sighed and picked up the handle of my antique white and gold phone.

"Hello?"

"Hey, Olivia."

"Hi..." I said, not recognizing the voice.

"Do you remember me?"

"I'm afraid not," I said in a friendly but reserved tone.

"It's your favorite guy from the party the other night," he said, and began laughing.

"How did you get my number?"

"Oh, Jaime gave it to me. I told him we really hit it off. He asked if it was an 'Indian thing.' That's when I told him I'm Mexican, though certainly I am Indian. Probably Aztec. Or Mayan. Who knows."

I sighed. "Are you a stalker?"

Tomás roared with laughter and half way through, I dropped the phone down into the receiver, knowing he would call back. Two minutes later, the phone rang.

"Yes," I said dully, picking up.

"This game is fun," he said. "And no, I'm not a stalker. I just like you. And I like teasing people. Is that so wrong?"

I switched the phone over to my shoulder and lay back. "I'm sure there's a plethora of girls just waiting for you to harass them. I assure you, they'll be much less trouble than I am. I only picked the phone up so as not to bother my daddy. "

He was silent for a moment. Then he said, "Say daddy again."

"You fool. Don't call again," I said, dropping the phone and smiling.

Tomás began to call regularly, a few hours after school let out. We didn't go to the same high school, so he knew that was the only way to make contact with me, to try to get me to meet up with him. For weeks, we'd play the same game; I would play coquette, he the teasing but anxious suitor, and I came to rely on those calls, look forward to them, even though I took every opportunity to hang up.

Finally, after a few weeks, he asked if we could meet. "Just for coffee."

"But you're a stalker. Won't I just be encouraging you?" I asked, laying on my bed. I usually lay down when I talked to him, the old springs of the daybed creaking heavily despite my small frame.

"Oh definitely. But I'll let you press charges if I start driving past your house. I'm generous like that. I mean, for a stalker."

"Fine," I said, trying to sound as bored as I possibly could, when my heart was speeding like a rabbit's. "I suppose."

Tomás laughed softly. "You're locked up so tight, Olivia. How can you breathe?"

"I manage just fine," I said, running my free hand over my bun.

"Well. I better stop before I lose my coffee date."

"Date. Who said anything about this being a date? This is merely coffee."

"OK, certainly. It's *merely* coffee," he said. "So don't make any large declarations of love on our first time having coffee. I know how demonstrative you are, and frankly, it's terrifying."

"Yes. That's me," I said, trying not to laugh, "I'm such an extrovert."

That weekend, I walked over to the diner around 7:00. Dad had been questioning me about the calls, and I kept telling him it was nothing, just a friend. He had looked at me suspiciously, his wild black eyebrows going up, and his long, thin mouth turning even further down. He was terrified that I would get pregnant, that I would ruin my chances of getting out, of having a better life. I had reassured him a million different times that I felt the same way, that I couldn't be bothered with boys, that I wasn't even interested in them, not at this point. But he could see something in my eyes that even I didn't want to see. Something I could see in the mirror every night, right before bed, after my long talks on the phone with Tomás. I would hang up, walk over to my tiny desk, and start in on my homework. But it didn't feel the same as it had before. I was restless, and I felt like a young, strange animal. A caged animal. Before bed, looking in the mirror, into my own wide black eyes I would wonder who the person was who had taken residency in my body. She was dangerous, and I didn't like her.

Tomás was already there, sitting up front. I felt a little weird having suggested the Denver Diner, as that was my dad's place and mine, but I liked it there and Tomás had seemed amenable. He had mentioned that he and the guys from his team often went there.

He smiled when he saw me, that sly little smile that somehow managed to convey sarcasm without a word.

"What are you so happy about?" I asked, slipping my pink and white jacket off, and sliding as elegantly as I could into a red, sparkling plastic booth.

"I think we both know the answer to that," he said and I shook my head and rolled my eyes slightly.

"I'm quite sure I'm the third girl you've seen today. Probably in this same restaurant. Probably even in this same booth." I put my hand down onto the plastic. "Shame shame. Still warm."

Tomás laughed and looked around for the waitress. She was already heading over to our booth. She smiled at me. I liked her. She looked as if she was somewhere in her mid-forties. She looked tired, her thin, brown hair up in a loose ponytail.

"Just coffee please. I doubt I'll be staying long."

Tomás cocked his head and gave me a pouty look. "So, I'm not the only one with other paramours on the books today?" he said and took a sip of his coffee.

"Hardly. I have loads of homework and then I go to the studio tomorrow."

"I see. I have you for some time?"

"For some time," I said, accepting the cup from the waitress, who had returned with my coffee.

The diner was going for that retro fifties thing, but mainly it was just dingy. I traced the edge of the fake silver rimmed countertops, my finger catching on a loose bit, the plastic flaking off easily.

"Tell me more about ballet. What drew you to it?"

I looked at him suspiciously and then took a sip of my coffee. "You really want to know?"

"Yes. I really really actually and truly want to know. I know you're an athlete. Remember, my mom's a dancer. Was a dancer."

"She quit?"

"You could say that, yes," Tomás said, looking uneasy and running a long brown hand through his hair. "She quit everything."

"Everything? How does one quit everything?"

"She met my father and she had me. And my dad wanted her to stay home and raise me while he worked. And getting pregnant wasn't exactly what one is supposed to do when one is a young dancer in a company."

"Hm," I said, not wanting to say what I really thought, which was that I didn't think very well of his father for impregnating his mother at such an important time in her life. "Well, you can't dance forever," I said, which was the best thing I could come up with.

"No. You can't," Tomás said, his voice lowering.

"Did your mom want to quit?"

"Yes and no. I mean, she met my dad while she was touring. And she was tired. And she was about to turn twenty, which as you know, is terribly old for a dancer. And the competition was so cruel, the women there were awful to her. The goal was to get on in a company in New York, and they were cutting each other's throats to do it. Not to mention that they did five evening shows a week, two matinees. And almost everyone she worked with was on coke. And she was just a kid from Peru who loved dancing and was good at it. And my dad is a sort of entrepreneur. He has a little chain of Mexican restaurants."

"Go on. Tell me a bit more and perhaps I'll tell you a little about myself. Just a little," I said, taking another sip of coffee and looking into his eyes. They were like mine, and yet nothing like mine. Black, slanted, but a different shape. And they had the same complications, but from a different source. It was strange to be thinking of a boy like this. I had always avoided it. And it was easy to. They were often so boring, so clearly only invested in the fact that I was pretty and thin, and I was only thin because it was what my art required. I found women who were thin just to be thin tremendously unattractive. And my body was taut with muscle, hard, athletic muscle. Muscle that was there for utilitarian, not cosmetic reasons. Frankly, I found my own naked body somewhat appalling when I looked at it from a purely aesthetic lens. But when I looked at it as instrument, I loved it deeply.

Tomás sighed. "Well...what other kind of David Copperfield kind of crap do you want to know?"

"Ha. Oh, just the usual. How they met. Did they love one another. Are they now filled with existential angst," I said, running my finger over the rim of my white, ceramic cup.

"Oh, they're definitely filled with existential angst. They're middle-class Latinos, so that's a given," he said and I thought that I would devote a little time to wondering about that later. "But as to how they met. Like I said, my mother was on tour. One of her stops was in Denver. And my father was doing well by that point. Ah – I forgot to mention that my father is much older than my mother. He's twenty years older, in fact," he said, running his hand through his hair again and pausing. He was so pretty, with his brown skin and high cheekbones, his slightly wavy black hair. He didn't dress like any other jock I knew, though runners were always a little different, a little classier. But even those guys generally wore some version of the high school jock uniform, the jersey or tee-shirt and jeans. But

Tomás was wearing a nice looking button down shirt, striped. And I could see his crisp, new-looking Navy Pea Coat tucked neatly beside him. He almost looked like a little baby businessman.

I tried to look nonplussed, after hearing that his father was years older than his mother, but frankly it disturbed me. I wondered if he could see that in my eyes and I wondered what else he could see in them, considering that he seemed to be able to manipulate me so well.

"So, in any case," he said, adjusting himself, "they met at a party."

"A party?" I said. This didn't seem to fit the profile of either one of them.

"Oh, not just any party. The kind of party wealthy people go to in this city. My father liked...likes to think of himself as a sophisticated man. Though he grew up with nothing. Ten billion siblings, parents illegal immigrants who worked in restaurants, you know, that whole story," he said nonchalantly.

"Yes. That whole story," I repeated.

"What? It is a Mexican story. And I know it's not a particularly interesting one. But it's his," he said, turning and looking deeply into the restaurant, his eyes clouding over. He looked back at me. "But my father has tried very hard to distance himself from all of that. He started a scholarship for Latinos, you know, for folks who want to go to college but don't have the money."

"Well, that's decent of him," I said.

"Yes. Decent. Though of course he hasn't seen his own family in years. There was some sort of big fight. He won't talk about it. And he doesn't like how close my mother is to her family."

I didn't like hearing that.

"Why?"

He sighed heavily. "I think because he wants to be her only focus. He's miserably in love with her, and he deals with it by being insanely possessive."

I frowned.

He smiled. "I know what you're thinking."

I tightened my mouth. Then I said, "I didn't know you were psychic. I'll have to watch my thoughts from here on out."

"Oh, you should. They're very dirty."

I rolled my eyes while he laughed.

"No, Olivia, I know what *any* woman would be thinking if she were told that this was what his father was like. That this is what the son is like. Let me assure you, I am far more like my mother than my father. For example, my father is very practical, and very intelligent. And hard working, obviously. But he is the least funny man I think I've ever met. And my mother is funny. And very nice, by the way. And she loves my father. She just...probably wishes that she hadn't married so early. And that he wasn't so jealous."

"I see," I said, sighing deeply.

"He does cheat though."

"Oh," I said. "How does your mother feel about that."

"Frankly, it's a relief for her. For at least while he's involved with someone else, the pressure is off of her. And she knows he'll always come back. And that he does it just to get her attention. It's all very telenovela."

I laughed. Those would come on sometimes in the afternoon, and I liked watching them. It would help me with my Spanish, and they were somehow more fun than the soap operas in English. There was more flare, more drama. More of a sense that they were a performance.

The waitress came back, steel carafe in hand. "More coffee?" She asked, and I nodded. Tomás also nodded and she poured.

"You mean I haven't scared you off?" he asked, and I could tell that through his confidence lay some fear.

"Well, you've scared me. But not scared me off. Yet."

"I see."

I drank from my cup and wondered what I was doing here, why it was that this person had gotten through when so many hadn't. I didn't think of myself as some sort of sacred object, no one could afford to look at themselves that way in my situation, but I did think of myself as an escape artist. And I had never let anyone get in the way of that. And this person could. I didn't like that.

"So this party," I asked, "for the wealthy. Where they met." I was interested in these kinds of things. They were the kinds of things that I wanted to be invited to someday, the kinds of parties where I felt I would meet the kinds of people who would appreciate me.

"Yes. Well, it was sort of an after-party, if you will. My mother was in Swan Lake and my father of course had front row seats. And an invite to the after-party. He said he was in love with her from the first step she made onto the stage, but then again, my father has a flair for the dramatic. And he drinks."

"Is he an alcoholic?" I asked, then wished I could take it back. But Tomás seemed unoffended.

"No. Actually, he really can't take his alcohol, which amuses my mother to no end, because even though she's not a huge drinker herself, she can drink practically anyone under the table."

"I like your mom already."

"Me too. She's my best friend. And she makes sure that my Spanish is on-point. We speak more in Spanish than in English, actually. Which is nice for me, because sometimes we travel, and I never have to feel left out."

"Do you travel to Peru?"

"Yes, and we visit my mother's family when my father isn't throwing a temper tantrum about it. My mother is very close to her mother and sisters. And they're very funny. And we drink and talk and walk to the ocean and swim. They live in Lima. Sometimes I think I want to move there, but I don't know what I'd do besides mooch off of them. And though they're not ridiculously poor, they're not in the kind of financial place where that would be a very nice thing to do. And they'd let me, because they love my mother, and therefore me."

"I bet they have a nickname for you," I said slyly.

He colored slightly. "Why...how do you...why do you ask that?"

"I don't know. I know that Natives do that. And...I just can tell that your aunties are the kind to do that. Come on. Tell me."

"Dear God. OK, on one, well two conditions," he said, looking deeply into my eyes, which was tremendously disconcerting. He leaned towards me. He smelled like sweet almonds, like I had always imagined my mother to smell like.

"What's that?" I asked. It was my turn to adjust in my seat.

"Well, that we finally talk about you. Because somehow you've gotten my entire life story out of me without telling me a thing about yourself."

"OK," I said. "We'll stop talking about you. But what's the second condition?"

"That you agree to have dinner with me and my mother next Saturday. It'll be fun. My father will be gone on business, and my mother and I always have wine and watch a movie and relax."

"You're asking me to meet your mother on the second date?" I said. I shifted again uncomfortably.

"Oh, this is a date now?" Tomás said. "I thought I told you not to make any large declarations of love but you're just so enamored of me, you just couldn't help yourself, could you?"

"Don't tease. Really, can't we meet her another time? I mean, meeting a parent is sort of, well, serious. And I barely know you. And hardly like you," I said, trying to lighten the mood.

"My mother is great, Olivia, you'll love her. And I promise. She won't think we're about to be married. She's very modern. And hip. You know, she's a dancer and you guys could talk dance. She's seen the world." He sat back and smiled at me mischievously. "Even if you spent the night, she wouldn't have a problem with it."

I looked at him indignantly. "If you think..." I started, and he quickly interrupted.

"I don't. But it's fun to tease you."

I sat back and contemplated him for a moment, and he didn't try to prod me. I liked that.

"OK. But only if it's nothing serious..."

"Relax. Babies on the third date," he said.

I couldn't help it, I smiled a little, though I tried desperately not to.

"OK. Now pay up. Nickname, please."

"Oh. Yeah. That. It's...well, it's guapito."

I died laughing. "Cutie. Little cutie pants. Little cutie from America," I said, in a slightly sing-songy manner. He reddened again.

"Yes. I guess it does directly translate to...cutie."

"Well, *guapito*, I've got to go."

"Hey! I thought you were going to tell me about yourself. That was part of the deal," he said, looking pouty.

"Next time. At your house. I'll give you all of that David Copperfield kind of crap."

He stood up with me. "You're very cruel you know. But of course, I like that in a woman."

"What a glutton for punishment," I said, putting on my coat.

"I'll give you a ride home," he said, slipping his coat on.

"That's not necessary. I live only two blocks away," I said, not wanting him to see the complex where I lived. It was old and shitty looking. And he was rich. And I wanted to keep him wanting. To keep him not knowing whether he had me or not.

"Really, Olivia, it's no trouble. It's cold."

"I like to walk," I said, heading for the door, Tomás behind me. I could feel the heat of his body behind me, and I tried my best to shrug it off, as if I'd had one too many glasses of red wine.

He was silent for a moment. "You know...I don't care where you live. I grew up well. But my parents didn't. And...so if...," he said awkwardly, struggling not to insult me.

It was my turn to color. "That's not it," I snapped, and then felt badly. That *was* it, and he knew it.

"I'm sure. But really, I'd love to."

"OK," I said softly, and he led me to his car. It was a new looking Subaru, and I stopped myself from saying something about it being a yuppie car. I hated it when I felt that kind of thing because in all honesty, I wanted those things. Badly. And acting like a class warrior would only keep me out.

On the way home, I was silent. I couldn't help but feel that I shouldn't have accepted his offer of a ride. I hardly knew him. And I didn't want him to see where I lived, however he felt about it. There was a certain kind of dignity I needed to maintain to the outside world, in order to make me feel like I was something that I wasn't, that I could be something else someday.

"It's here," I said, and Tomás pulled over. "And you don't need to pull close, I can get out here."

He sighed heavily and he turned to me, compassion in his eyes. "No. No way Olivia. I don't want you to think I'm the kind of guy who drops a girl off and doesn't walk her to her door."

I was silent again.

"Please. I want to walk you to your door. I don't care what kind of a door it is," he said and I could hear the anxiety in his voice.

"I just..."

"I know. But Olivia, if you could only see where my mother's family lives in Peru. And I like it there! And you're special. Please, let me treat you that way."

"OK," I said, and he slid into a parking spot. I opened the door as he was coming around and smiled awkwardly. He had been coming around to open the door for me.

He smiled back and I led the way.

"Thank you," I said.

He placed his hand on the small of my back lightly and briefly, and I shuddered. When we got to the stairs that led to my door, I paused. "Really, this is far enough."

He cocked his head, looking at me with an expression of pure exasperation. "Olivia, you've come so far. Let me take you to your door."

I felt something screaming inside then, screaming in frustration. I didn't want to believe this person, I couldn't. I couldn't let him in. Not only because I was afraid he would hold me back, but because I feared he would unlock something that I had kept buried for as long as I could remember. And if I let it out, what would I be then? And what if he took it from me?

"OK," I said petulantly and he followed me up the stairs.

At the door, he paused. "Well, goodnight. And see you Saturday. How about I pick you up? At 6:00?"

"Sure. That would be great," I said, already feeling nervous. I felt already that I wouldn't be enough, that his mother would find me lacking.

"My mother will love you," he said, briefly touching my arm.

"OK...*guapito*," I said and he closed his eyes briefly.

"I really wish you hadn't gotten that out of me. You have special powers."

"Goodnight," I said and opened the door.

"Goodnight," he said back, and I could feel his presence outside even as I closed it.

That night, I lay back on my bed, and thought about Tomás. Dad had been sitting by the TV, asleep, his big head lolling back into the couch, his hand curled around a half-finished beer like a kitten. I had smiled and taken the can from his hand and dumped the remainder in the sink, and thrown it into the trash. I didn't want to wake him, because he looked so deeply asleep, his face like a gorgeous old bull's. I had tucked an old pink and blue afghan around him and gotten ready for bed as quietly as possible.

I felt conflicted. Almost angry even. I had designed an impervious fortress, and somehow Tomás was gently breaking it down. I could picture it in my mind, that fortress, and I often did. It was a castle with a moat. A long, wide deep moat, that contained all kinds of mysterious monsters. Beyond it was everyone I feared being, the girls with babies in their arms, cooing over the soft faces of the children that only meant their destruction. The first one was at fifteen. The second, seventeen. By the time they were in their thirties, they looked ancient, their children clinging to them in the grocery stores like so many demented animals, their faces slack, devoid of humanity, of life. Or they were filled with a kind of stupid rage, striking their children back from the cart, from their arms, from the miles and miles of breakfast cereal in the aisles. The kids would look hurt, then try again, their arms around their heads, blocking the inevitable blow. I had determined to never be like that. Just thinking about it made me shudder, but I often did to remind myself of what happened when people let their emotions get the better of them, when they didn't think about their futures, when they let the people around them tell them they were nothing without a man, when they let those men control them. I felt revulsion at their simpering faces, their baby-voices developed especially for boys, their constant need for approval from boys who were much more interested in getting it from each other. I watched boys sometimes, and though I respected the jocks for what they were doing, their constant verbal and physical horseplay made them look stupid, vulnerable. And the way they treated their girlfriends, or the girls that surrounded them was abhorrent. I liked being able to control them, to flirt with them, to make them want me and yet never, ever show any vulnerability. I never answered the phone. I never stayed long in a conversation, and I always flirted with the edge of a promise, but I never promised anything, and I certainly didn't deliver. This wasn't because I was a good girl, those girls disgusted me more than anyone, the ones who held their virginity up as if it were some sort of prize. What my father didn't know, what nobody knew, was that I had been on birth control for years, and had on occasion, gotten into a few of the nicer bars downtown and had had sex with a number of men. I knew that it was important that I understood these kind of men, these men in expensive grey suits, with expensive haircuts, bored with their expensive wives that they treated like any other thing that they had bought. But I could see what would make them vulnerable, what I could do to control them. They were bored, their expressions of desperation so close under their skin, it made me laugh. And because my look was sophisticated, and my features very mature, I was never turned away from a bar, or turned away from a man. I was light-skinned enough to look exotic and whenever I was asked about my ethnicity I told them I was European, and they would nod, as if this were not the most obvious fabrication in the world. I liked them married, because rarely was there a sense that they would get attached, though I'd seen one married man who I particularly liked for a while, until I was sick of him. I wasn't afraid of sex. I was afraid of pregnancy and I was afraid of being vulnerable. Something about Tomás made me feel like I was surging out of control, that he had untapped a dam inside me, and that I didn't know what I would do once the water had pushed past every gate that I had worked so hard to put up. I decided that when I woke up, I would call him and cancel for Saturday. There was nothing I could learn from him that would help me get out of here. He could only keep me back.

Every day after work, I picked up the phone, and put it down.

"You seem strange lately," Dad said. He was making me breakfast.

"How so?" I asked.

"You seem like you're always thinking about something... someone."

I laughed. "Oh, daddy, you know how I feel about boys," I said, smoothing my robe. It was a silky pink one that I'd found in the thrift store one Saturday. I adored it. I hoped it made me look older.

"Yes, I know," he said, putting a fork in a sausage.

He was silent then, and I knew he knew I was lying.

"I find them all so booooring. Except for you, of course."

He sighed and pushed the eggs around in the pan.

"You know I'm just scared for you. I want you to get out of here."

"Daddy, we're of one mind here, you know that. I'm much more interested in ballet and taking French and just about anything beyond *boys*. They're all children anyway! I mean, if you could only see the boys that I know in school..." I said, trailing off, knowing that I was going on, knowing that I would go to Tomás' that night, grateful with the knowledge that daddy was working the late shift. All I had to do was tell him that I was going to the coffee shop to study after dinner, and then I'd be scot-free. I nearly hated Tomás.

Daddy finished the sausages and eggs and made a plate for me. I already had a large cup of coffee in front of me, and moved it aside to make room. I picked at it, trying to eat a bit more than I normally would to make daddy happy.

"How is school?" He asked, shoveling bite after bite in. He was like a machine that one, and he needed to fuel up because he was huge, and he worked long, hard hours with very few breaks.

"I'm doing really well. A's on nearly everything, of course. And I love my French class. It makes me feel like I'm living in a fairy tale when I speak it; it really does."

Daddy nodded, but I could tell he was sad, and I felt like tearing up. I knew that he knew me better than anyone else, in fact, no one knew me really except for daddy, and I kept so much from him. I took a sip of my coffee and asked him if he wanted to go to the thrift store today. He smiled.

The day was nice, the snow had mainly melted into grey and daddy and I took the bus to our favorite thrift store. I wandered the aisles, my hand brushing the dusty shoulders of the shirts I was walking past. I stopped. Looked at a few shirts absentmindedly and moved on. My heart wasn't in it. Then I thought about my dinner with Tomás and his mother and I thought to get something new, something relatively new at least. I was lucky being so thin, because though I could never afford to clothe myself in the latest, there were often a few nice pieces in my sizes, and I hunted for them. I went over to the dresses and began to go through them, one by one. The majority of what was there was awful; things from the 70's that looked like they'd spent their lives in a dryer mildewing after too many wears on a woman exhausted from too many chores around the house.

I didn't like things that were contemporary. I liked things with a classic look, things that looked good on me. The huge shoulder pads and garish colors so popular in the 80's were things that I generally avoided. They looked wrong on me anyway. I liked pale colors and clothing that flowed around me, rather than constricted. A girl at school had turned to me in Algebra class once, her large golden hoops swinging slightly and her bright pink lips parting to tell me, "If I was as skinny as you was, I'd wear things as tight as I could find them." "Thanks," I had told her and she had turned back to her notebook, which was filled with doodles surrounding a boy's name.

I pulled a pink dress out from the rest, but it was too large, and there were too many worn spots. I put it back and continued. There was a spot of yellow up ahead that intrigued me. I pulled that dress out and looked at it, at the label, the size. But it was so short. As much as I hated to admit it, I didn't want Tomás' mother to think ill of me. And I generally didn't like short things anyway, my legs were so thin, they didn't look very good unless I wore tights, ending in toe shoes. I went through the aisle, all the way up, and found myself disappointed. I went back over to the men's section, to find daddy, to see if he was ready to go, but he was busily trying on all kinds of shoes, sitting in the aisle like a kid. I laughed and told him I would be in the women's clothing section. I decided to look in the aisle where all of the skirts were. Sometimes there were a few nice skirts, something from the 50's or 60's that was cut in a classic, A-line shape. But there was nothing. A few cheap Madonna pseudo-ballet skirts in neon and black, more horrifying things from the 70's, their colors like a psychedelic monster of some sort had vomited all over something often in the shape of flowers. I went over to the shirts, and found a few I liked, a few plain tee-shirts in colors I didn't find too garish. I went back over to see if daddy was done, but he was no longer in the shoe section. I walked around looking for him and found him in the section where all of the kitchen stuff was kept. He was looking at a microwave. It looked old, the brown paint on the dials mainly worn off, but not in bad shape. Daddy had kept saying that he wanted to get one, just to warm things up here and there. He was a good cook, though he cooked mainly basic things, so I had been surprised when he first mentioned it.

I walked up to him. "What did you find?"

"This," he said, opening the door and looking in. "Though I don't know if it still works. The girl up at the front said that it did but they always say that."

"Tell her you want to test it out."

"Yeah. Yeah, that's a good idea. Do you mind waiting?"

"Of course not. I'll just go look at the dresses again."

I walked back over to the dresses, thinking again about Tomás and his mother. I couldn't believe that he'd asked me out for a second date with his mother. This really was either a very good or a very bad sign. I sighed and brushed my hand against the dresses. I hated that he made me feel this way, think these kinds of things. And I didn't need another dress, I just wanted one, because this felt...special. And many of my dresses were very sophisticated, because I bought them to look much older than I was, for all of my interludes at the various expensive bars I went to, looking to find men. I thought then that this might be the solution to my problem. I could tell Tomás about my exploits, and he'd be horrified and let me be. But the very thought turned my stomach. I didn't want things getting out and maybe even getting to my father. As much as I found the whole good girl/bad girl thing to be preposterous, and frankly, boring, I knew my father would be hurt. And sad. And worried. And disappointed. Additionally, I liked that no one knew about it. I liked that it was part of a private life I had, that no one could touch. And I was very safe, not only had I been on birth control for years, but I always used a condom, and I always carried a small knife my father had given me. I kept it in the leather sheath he'd given it to me in, and I kept that in my bra, which I never ever took off, telling them that I was self-conscious about my breasts. They always begged and whined for me like puppies to remove it but when they kept on, I would start to get out of bed, and they would calm down and stop asking. I laughed a little in the dress aisle, thinking about how easy they were to control. Then I thought about Tomás and went silent.

I walked over to the section where most of the white dresses were and pulled each one out. Most were frilly, old-fashioned. A few were of course, loaded down with shoulder pads, as if the women wearing them were readying for war. I sighed and looked over at daddy. He had gotten the woman at the front to allow him to take the microwave to a plug in the back and he was plugging it in now. I shook my head and turned back to the dresses. I pulled one after another out, until I found what I was looking for. It was simple, it was my size, and it was in lovely shape. And it wasn't too short or frilly. I pulled it out and walked over to the overcrowded dressing room and stood in line. When it was finally my turn, I tried the tee-shirts on I'd picked up earlier, and then the dress. I was happy. It worried me that it was white, because not only was the connotation virginal, it was also marital, and I really didn't want to signify either. But it was nice, simple. And cotton, which I loved. Synthetic material always looked cheap as far as I was concerned and it also wore away quickly in the spots you least wanted it to. Satisfied, I walked up to the cashier and paid and then went up to the front where there were a few old chairs. I sat down on an aging orange and black chair and thought about how I wished daddy would let me have a job like everyone else in school, but he wanted me to focus on school and on ballet. It always made me feel weird when he handed me money, as if I were a child from a middle-class home with an allowance. At least my needs were very few. I went to the coffee shop when I went out at all. And ballet had gotten less expensive for me over the years, as my teacher had lowered the price so that I could afford to take it several times a week. She believed in me. And I still loved to dance, and that was wonderful. Wednesday, in class, we had been practicing a complicated combination with several pirouettes, and though my feet hurt and I was exhausted, I was determined to do it right. My teacher was smart. I knew she favored me but she never let on. She knew that kind of behavior could ruin a dancer. But of course I knew she did, after all, she had lowered the price years ago, and had given me the keys to the studio to practice on my own. There had been a moment, spinning, where I felt almost as if I had transcended my body, I felt like light, like something that lived far away from this earth. I had to catch myself, because I knew that it was making me want to close my eyes, and that was the last thing that you wanted to do in ballet. I looked up and daddy was standing above me, the microwave in his hands, a gigantic smile on his lips.

"Five dollars! And it works like a charm. I tested it out," he said, as I got out of the chair and dusted myself off.

"That's great dad."

"I've been looking for a good one for a year now. I can't believe someone donated this."

We made our way over to the bus station and waited, daddy crading the microwave in his arms like a baby.

On the way home, I was quiet, but dad hardly noticed, as he was going on about how we could use the microwave. When we got home, I walked to my room and set my new dress down on my bed. It smelled musty and I told daddy that I was going to go down to the Laundromat to do laundry. He barely nodded, as he was busy clearing a space for the new microwave. I smiled and shook my head, told him that I'd see him tomorrow. He mumbled something like, "Love you," as I walked out the door.

After I'd washed the clothes, and came home, I got down on my knees by my bed and extended my arm into the darkness underneath, fishing for the little bottle of bourbon I kept for special occasions. I rarely drank, but I liked bourbon, and when I felt like it, when daddy wasn't home, I sometimes had a finger. I didn't want to worry him. He'd told me once that mom had liked to drink, a lot. I looked in the mirror and thought about what make-up I should wear.

I picked up a tube of light pink lipstick from my dresser and sighed. Sometimes I pictured my mom like one of those old-fashioned noir women from a French film. All red lips and red nails and cruelty. A woman who lives in dives, who sings in them, who makes tragic but glamorous decisions about her life. Who tells the men in her life off, even when they're in love with her. Especially when they're in love with her. I turned the tape player on, the one I kept on my dresser by my make-up bag. The tape was a copy of something my teacher had played for us one Saturday at the studio. It was something kind of modern and sad. It made me shudder.

I looked at the clock. It was 5:30. I had thirty minutes. I pulled on some stockings, the white dress and a pair of pink flats. I looked down at them, wondering if the color was too bold and hating myself for caring. They were light pink. Then I thought of course about the snow, and how cold it would be walking from the apartment to the car, and I slipped them off. I went back to the closet and looked through all of the boots I'd found at the thrift store. There was a pair of beige boots, with just a kitten heel that seemed appropriate. And they were decently warm. Of course, they were quite worn in the heel and had been when I'd bought them. But they were passable. And not too bold. I went back over to the mirror to finish my make-up.

When I was done, I got my purse and jacket from the closet and sat down on my couch, the music from the tape playing out into the living room. I looked over at the new microwave. It had a digital clock set into it and dad had set it. It was 5:50. I settled into my chair and tried to relax. *He was a child. He was only a child. A gorgeous sophisticated child...*

There was a knock at the door and I started. He was early. I walked over to the door, peered out through the peep hole and saw that it was Tomás. He was smiling that sly, sarcastic little smile of his and staring directly at the peep hole. I opened the door and he walked in.

"Well, aren't you little Mr. Early," I said and closed the door.

"Yes, I'm very punctual. You'll find that it's one of the many, sexy, sexy things about me. That and I always say thank you."

He looked at me and cocked his head. "You look nice," he said, and though I colored, I tried to act nonchalant. He looked nice as well, and he smelled good.

He looked into the living room. "Is that a barre affixed to your wall?" He asked, walking over to it and running his hand along the surface.

"Yes. Daddy...dad, put that up for me, and did the floors as well."

He turned to me. "That's incredibly sweet," he said, and my heart began to hammer in my chest.

He walked over to the chair where I'd laid my coat and picked it up, held it open for me. I walked over and let him help me slip into it, his breath on my neck.

"Well. Should we be off?"

"Yes," he said, looking at me.

"What?"

"You know," he said, and I felt a shudder pass through me.

"I don't know anything," I said and he leaned in and kissed me, softly, briefly, his hand on the small of my back for just a moment.

On the drive to Tomás' house, we began to laugh, to joke around. I began to relax, but when we pulled into the drive, I became nervous again. His house wasn't a mansion per se, but it was so much bigger than my place, it was like it was. Sometimes when I went home with different men, they had houses like this. I often tried to imagine what it would be like to live in one.

Tomás came around and opened the door for me.

"Hey mom," he yelled as we walked in. A lovely, thin brown woman came around the corner and smiled.

"So good to finally meet the girl Tomás has been going on and on about," she said and came over to me and gave me a brief hug.

"Not that that isn't true, but try not to humiliate me right off the bat," he said and she laughed and led us into the kitchen.

We sat and talked while she finished dinner. There was a plate of cheese and a bottle of opened wine and Tomás poured me a glass. I was relieved to find that his mother was kind, funny and not snotty at all. We talked and shared stories all throughout dinner, and then went into the living room to talk more and drink more wine.

"Yes, Tomás always thinks he's so funny," his mother said. Her name was Diana, and it was a perfect name for such a woman. She was exactly as I hoped I would be someday, minus the emotionally needy husband.

"Well, I try," he said, "and mom always lets me know when I've failed."

"You have to keep a boy in check," she said, pouring a bit more for all of us. "They are arrogant so easily. And there is nothing more boring than an arrogant man."

I nodded and told her that I agreed. She was wearing a long, expensive looking dress that somehow seemed to look casual and formal all at once, and yet she had not looked askance at my thrift store dress and had even told me how lovely I looked.

"Oh, mom, you'd keep the whole world in check if you could," he said, shaking his head. He seemed to not only take her in stride, but enjoy her.

"The world is too much work. In any case, Tomás, if you are to take this girl home in one piece, you should have a glass of water. I'm getting tired. And I'm sure this one has a curfew," she said, and looked in my direction.

"Actually...my father doesn't know I'm here," I said, awkwardly. I took a sip of wine.

"No?" Diana asked, looking confused.

"Well, he doesn't want me around boys. He just worries for me, you know." And then I realized what that implied and felt myself coloring deeply.

"Ahhh, yes. My parents were very strict as well. I understand. You want to dance, and he knows that will help you in this world. Well, I can assure you, my little Tomás is a very good boy. I'm sure he wants you to get everything in this world you deserve. In fact," she said, standing up, "one more drink to that, to everyone getting what they work for."

We clanked glasses and I began to feel better, though when I looked over at Tomás I could see that he had a very strange expression on his face.

On the way home, he was strangely pensive, silent. I told him that I liked his mother, and he nodded.

"So, which schools have you applied to?" he asked.

"Only a few in New York. My teacher assures me that I'll get into one of them."

He was silent again for a moment and then said, "I see."

"How about you?" I asked.

"Oh. Just local schools. Regis. DU. University of Colorado at Boulder."

"Those are great schools," I said and he was silent again.

When he pulled up to my complex and parked, he smiled. "Can I walk you to your door?" He asked. He seemed in a better mood.

"Sure," I said, my heart beginning to race, the wine heavy in my head. "Since little Tomás is such a good boy."

He groaned and got out, walking around the car and opening the door for me. I had waited for him this time.

We walked up to my apartment and I let him in.

"So, my father isn't getting home until 5:00 in the morning," I said, and he leaned in and kissed me. I took his hand and led him to my bedroom. I had decided not to fight it anymore.

After, he asked me if I smoked. "Here and there," I said, getting up and going to my dresser. I dug far back into my underwear drawer and pulled a pack of Marlboro's out.

We got dressed and walked outside. We sat and smoked and it was peaceful and cold, the complex mainly asleep, except for the couple that always argued. They lived on the first floor and were in a near-perpetual state of fury.

We giggled listening to them and then Tomás sighed, deeply.

"You know I'm sure one of the schools in Denver has a dance program, a ballet program."

"Sure," I said, exhaling, "but all of the good ones are in New York."

He was silent. Then, "I'm already a little attached to you, you know. Being a stalker, that's part of our job description."

A wave of mild shock came over me then. I realized that he wanted me to stay. That he thought we could be together. As in, perhaps permanently.

"Tomás..."

"Don't say it. I know. We're very young. But I know a good thing when I see it," he said, taking a drag, exhaling and then leaning over to kiss me.

"I do like you," I said, after he'd pulled away.

"Let me just leave it at that," he said. "I don't want to pressure you. I know we've just started to get to know one another," he got up, put his cigarette out and tossed it into the snow-covered ground below. He put his hand on my shoulder and I smiled. I got up, and he was silent, looking out into the night.

"I know I have to go," he said, "but just remember Olivia, these things don't come around all the time."

I leaned over and kissed him and watched him walk down the stairs, get into his car. I finished my cigarette and started a new one. It was my turn to look out into the night. The stars were bright. I looked up and into them, and into everything I'd promised myself. I didn't understand why Tomás was so anxious, so young. Why he wanted so much from me, when he'd really just started to get to know me. I liked him but I knew that I wouldn't let anyone stop me from going to New York. And I couldn't imagine him going with me. He clearly liked it here, clearly wanted to stay near his mother. Normally, I would have found that creepy, but she was wonderful. I wanted to stay with my dad too. But I knew that there was so much ahead of me, and there wasn't anything else I really loved, besides dance. I didn't want to do anything else, and I was good, very good. I could be something that other people couldn't. All of this filled me with sadness, with confusion, and when I finished my second cigarette, I went to sleep with images of my father, of Tomás, and of a future moving through my head like a cloud of bright blue cosmic dust.

"DON'T YOU CONDESCEND TO ME, YOU..."

"What. You what? You think you're so strong Olivia, but you are still a little girl who thinks every man is her daddy."

I ran up to him then, and he took my wiry yellow arms in his hands and crushed them to his chest. I pulled them free and walked into our bedroom. Things had gotten bad. David kept telling me that I was getting older, and that he was impatient for me to settle down, to start a studio in New York. But I was twenty-six and I knew that my career could not be over, that I could keep touring now that I was too old to be what I had been in New York for a few brief years. I knew that what David wanted was a wife.

I sat down on our bed and David followed. He sat down next to me and I felt like jumping out the window to get away from him.

"Olivia, I love you. But you can't expect me to wait forever. And you can't be that impervious."

I continued my silence, looked to my favorite painting. I had told David that it was my favorite. He said that the painting often made him sad. When I asked him why he kept it in his bedroom, he told me that he supposed he liked to keep things that made him sad close to him. I had rolled my eyes.

"Olivia, this silent treatment, it is like what a child does. You are only proving my point," he said, getting up and standing in front of me. "And it is time to grow up, stop pretending you are so tough. And soon you will be too old to tour even. You already are. And you are not that tough, and I'm sick of this, what is that stupid word, ghetto-routine."

I looked up at him in anger and then away.

He sighed deeply. "We should start dinner. I'm hungry. We can talk more about this later." He began to walk out of the bedroom door. I stopped him.

"You have no idea what I've been through. What I'm capable of," I said and something in my tone made David pause.

"What do you mean by that?"

"I love to dance. I gave up everything to dance. That is something you can never understand. Your mother danced, you grew up with money. You grew up with everyone applauding your every artistic move. I gave up everything, everything. And so don't you tell me that I have to stop dancing before I'm ready. I'm still young. I have until thirty and not a goddamn thing will stop me from eeking every bit of beauty out of my life before that part of it is over. And you can wait."

David was silent. His steely blue-grey eyes looking at me, into me, his hands listless at his sides. "I don't think that's what you really want Olivia. I've seen your softness."

I laughed then, hard and David began to shake his head.

"You want to know how hard I am? Remember Rome? Remember when I asked you if you wanted children and you told me that there was plenty of time? I was pregnant then David. You idiot. And I got rid of it."

The look of horror on David's face was something that I hadn't expected.

"You...you whore."

Tremendous satisfaction rolled all the way through me, like a wave. "Yes, that's right. I'm a whore, every woman's a whore."

"No, just you. Just you are a whore," David said, turning and walking out.

I sat on the bed for a long time, listening to David cry in the kitchen, feeling like something evil, like something that had emerged out of a cave. A great black and silver thing, not of this world. Something born on another planet, maybe Mars. I saw myself in this cave, living off of my own pain and anger and I didn't care. David was weak, they were all so weak. I felt a tightness in my chest and stomach that would never unwind, it was a part of my creature-ness, a part of my evil and it fed me. I was something born without a mother.

MY ROOMMATE WAS OUT WHEN I GOT THE CALL. It was one of my aunties, and she was crying. I looked out of the window of my apartment. The sun was shining. It was almost always shining in New Mexico. There were birds, and they were talking. I felt faint. I sat down to listen to her say it in her lilting Oklahoma accent.

"Have to go," I said faintly, dropping the phone and not bothering to put it on the hook. I could hear my auntie calling my name in the background, but it felt like I had suddenly been sunk under thousands of miles of ocean, like I was suddenly upside down, and as I made my way to the toilet, lurching from side to side like a broken toy, I began to tear at my arms and wail, and I vomited on the floor before I could even get to the bathroom.

An hour later, after I had gotten the pint of cheap vodka out of the kitchen, and crawled into bed with it, my roommate came in, though I didn't hear her until she got to the bedroom.

"Olivia, are you crying?" She asked. I looked at her, trying to answer. "There's vomit on the floor and the phone was off the hook, what's...oh, oh God, it's your father isn't it? Oh, God." She went to me and held me as I shook and cried. She pet my hair and tried to take the vodka from me. After some time, she got up and I could hear her cleaning the floor. Could hear her in the kitchen. She came in with soup and I shook my head.

"Olivia, you must eat. And I'm taking the vodka. Have some water, too," she said, and I let her take the vodka. I had been crying for so long, I had begun to go numb. And then it would start all over again, the pain.

I took the glass of water out of her hand, and then the soup and let her pet my head while I ate and drank, though it felt like my throat was closing up with every bit of liquid I tried to force down. She took my hand and led me to the living room and turned on the TV. She wrapped me in a blanket, my daddy's Pendleton that he'd given me when I went away to college, and let me cry, and then finally sleep.

Daddy had been at the hospital, mopping the floors, when a man had come in. They hadn't seen the gun. When he pulled it out, as they began to wheel him towards surgery, people screamed and daddy dropped his mop and walked over to see what was going on, to see if he could help. Daddy was always one to help. He was well liked on the job. The man began waving the gun, and it went off.

My roommate called Dancing Earth, my studio, and told them what had happened, and they were very sympathetic. I took two weeks, during which time I went home for Daddy's funeral. They were going to bury him in Oklahoma, in Ada, where he'd been born. I wondered if my mother would show up, but nobody knew where she was, and though I looked around for a woman who looked like me at the funeral, a tall light-skinned woman standing on a little yellow hill, dressed in black, there was no one like that, and I went home soon after.

For a long time, I merely functioned. Days would go by and I'd realize that I had lost my sense of time completely. My roommate had to make me eat, and I grew thinner than I'd ever been. If she wasn't there to make me, I just didn't. That tightness in my throat was always there, and I was putting off going back to Denver to get daddy's things. I knew that I needed to, that the landlord had put things in storage for me, but that it was ridiculous to continue to pay the rent for storage for furniture I didn't need. I just couldn't stand the idea of going through his things, of throwing his whole, tiny life away. He had been all I'd really had. The last time I'd visited him, he looked tired. His hair was white. He'd asked me why I wouldn't move home, and I'd told him that there were more opportunities in Albuquerque, but that was a half-truth. Coming home would be admitting my final defeat. When I told David that I'd gotten rid of our child, he became listless, uncaring. I had moved out soon after, to live with a number of dancers like when I'd first moved to New York and I'd continued to tour. But he had ultimately been right. A few years after that, the gigs began to dry up, and the idea of staying in New York, that city that had held so much magic for me once, was too much to bear, and I had packed my things and moved to Albuquerque. I entered the graduate program in dance there and completed it easily.

It took a long time before I was ready to go back up to Denver, go through daddy's things. I had decided, though I wasn't conscious of it at the time, that I would never go back. I had returned to work a few weeks after his death but the months that had passed since had been so bad that I felt like I was looking at things through a badly lighted tunnel most days.

I had booked a Motel 6 near the storage unit. I planned on getting it all done in a few days, and taking back what I could with me in my little car. The rest would be donated to the thrift store, the same thrift store daddy and I had loved to shop in on Saturdays.

The drive took around seven hours, hours in which I cried, played music, thought about how angry I was that daddy's life had been taken so brutally, in a way that had no meaning. I had wanted daddy to see me really grow up, turn my life around, and right before daddy had been shot, I thought perhaps I was finally on the brink of that. I was thirty-two. Things had begun to shift inside me, I had been cutting out the booze, the weeping, the stupid boys. I had been thinking about what I wanted to do with the rest of my life. When I had been young, all I could think about was making it as a dancer. It was as if I thought I would die after I couldn't dance anymore. When David would talk about having children, owning a studio, making a life, all I could feel was irritation, as if he didn't care about me, only what I could do for him. And something else; a deep feeling inside me that he was not the one I wanted to do those things with.

I pulled up to the Motel around 5:00, parked, checked in and went to the Denny's across the way. I wanted to go to the Denver Diner, but I was tired, and I knew it would make me too sad. I didn't like showing any emotion in public. I didn't like showing emotion.

The Denny's was busy with the dinner crowd, children crying and squealing, squirming in their seats, throwing their food. I ate my salad mechanically, the world around me alternately speeding up and then slowing down. I looked at the faces of the parents. Often, those faces were very tired. The mother's especially. It was as if they were there only to serve their children's needs. Often, the dads would only insert themselves if there was noise. Otherwise, they seemed content to let their wives deal with everything else. I paid my ticket and left.

I thought I would have trouble sleeping, as there had been many sleepless nights in the past few months, but I drifted off easily,after setting my copy of *Vanity Fair* on the nightstand.

The next day was bright, and I sighed as I sat up. After my shower, I went again to the Denny's and ordered a cinnamon roll and coffee. I had a sweet tooth. I had gotten that from daddy. I drove over to the unit, talked to the man, whose look of pity made me almost tearful, and we walked over to daddy's tiny unit.

"The landlord was nice. He threw away some trash for you," the man said. He was an old, scruffy looking white guy, and he smelled like sour beer, the kind of smell you sweat out after a night of drinking.

"Thanks," I said.

Going through the unit was hard. There was really so little. It was all about going through boxes and finding the things that were valuable to me personally. But it was also the little things: the erasers, the scraps of paper, the buttons we'd gotten at Denver March that said "I'm Indian and I Vote!" the tiny bits and pieces of his life that I knew had to be thrown away, but with every tiny thing he had squirreled away in a drawer somewhere that ended up in one of the giant sacks I'd brought for the dumpster, I felt like I was tossing his life away, who he had been further into the abyss.

I broke for lunch, which was a handful of almonds I'd brought with me. I sat on the couch that daddy and I had sat on so many times watching TV. Daddy liked comedies. He liked to laugh, and his laugh always made me feel better, closer to the earth, more human. Even as a child I had felt the monster growing inside me, the thing that needed out, away, that thing that people loved but didn't like.

As the light began to die, I looked over at the small sea of boxes. I was almost done. I had found some of my things, and a few of daddy's that I wanted to keep. Some items that I wanted to send to relatives. I had brought a few boxes with me and had packed them in. There was only one box to go, and tomorrow morning a truck from the thrift store was scheduled to come. I would be gone by then.

I opened the last box and sifted through loads of paper, mainly drawings I'd done when I was a child, notes I'd left for him, papers I recognized from the drawers of my dresser. I put most of it in the trash, keeping a piece or two. I'd almost reached the bottom of the box, when I found something with Tomás' name on it and froze. I put the paper in my bag and threw the rest of the papers in the box away, shut the storage unit door and went back to the hotel, my stomach grumbling. I sat in the hotel room, eating almonds mechanically and staring at the TV, even though I hadn't turned it on.

I pulled the heavy phone book out of the drawer of the nightstand and set it down in front of me on the bed. I opened it, and went through, looking under "T." There it was. Tomás Trujillo. If it was him. My finger paused over his name and I began to feel nervous, strange. Why call now? After all these years. After what happened. I could always bring this number with me to Albuquerque, sit on it. After all, my life was about to change. I would be moving soon. Did I really need to be drudging the past up, after all that had happened?

I dialed the number slowly, my long, skinny fingers pushing each button down as deliberately as possible. I laughed as the ringing began because I was treating this like it was a sacred act.

"Hello?"

"Tomás?"

It was him. It was his voice. I was sure of it.

"Yes?"

"This is Olivia. Olivia James."

I thought it would take him a while to recognize me, but it didn't.

He laughed softly. "Olivia. I knew you'd call someday."

"Oh did you?" I said coyly, easily falling back into our old routine.

"I did."

I started crying then.

"Oh, Olivia, what's wrong?"

"My dad. He died."

"I'm so sorry Olivia. I understand. My dad died two years ago, and as much as he was an old angry coot, I was sad as hell. Can I do anything?"

"No. No, thank you though. I just went through his storage unit. It was awful."

"I'm sure."

"You still have your mom though?" I asked, wishing I could get up and get a tissue from the bathroom. I shifted around the bed uncomfortably and thought about all the times I'd talked to him while sitting on my bed. How lovely that had been.

"Oh yes. She's still around. And still a glamorous creature of untold depths."

I laughed. "Oh, Tomás, you...you sound like you."

"I hope so," he said.

I thought about asking him to get together for breakfast.

"She just loves the kids. Though when we try to stick her with babysitting, she informs us that she's more than a babysitter," he said, laughing again.

It was as if he'd blown ice into me, through the phone. "Oh, you have kids? How many?" I asked, hoping I sounded normal. But I felt sick. I suppose there was a part of me that had been hoping...

"Two. And a dog and three cats. My wife's really into cats. She's like the neighborhood cat lady, though she's married and doesn't smell like cat piss."

I tried to laugh but all that came out of my mouth was an awkward choking noise.

"So, how long are you in town for? Would you like to come over for dinner tomorrow night? My wife's a terrible cook, but I'm not. My mother made sure I knew how to make every Peruvian dish in existence I think, much to my father's chagrin."

"Oh, maybe next time. I have to get back. I live in Albuquerque now," I said.

"Yeah. I know," he said, and his voice was strange.

"Oh," I said.

"Well, do you have to get back to work, or could you call in? I'd love to see you," he said.

"I have to get back because actually, well, I'm moving to Chicago."

"Chicago?"

"Yes. I have my master's now. And, well, I'm too old to be a professional. I've wandered around enough and, well, I applied to some universities and I'm going to be a teacher at a university there. Tenure-track."

"That's wonderful," he said, though he sounded sad.

"So, I'm exhausted," I said. "I really have to sleep."

"Sure, sure...but, Olivia, let's keep in touch, OK? Please call again."

"Of course," I said, and hung up.

I'M EIGHTEEN! I'm not going to *settle down*, are you insane?" I screamed.

We were in the parking lot. We had just graduated, and I was late for a dinner with my dad at the Denver Diner.

"Olivia, I love you! And I've accepted that you're going to New York. All I'm saying is that I want to be with you, that I want to wait. I can wait, Olivia."

I put my hand on the door handle. "I'm late."

Tomás sighed deeply and said, "I don't understand why you won't even tell your dad about me. We're having a big party at my house. I told you both of you should come."

"And I told *you* that my daddy doesn't approve of me going out with boys. He doesn't like the very idea–"

"You're eighteen years old. I'm a good boyfriend. From a good family. It's not like I'm some sort of..."

I looked over at him, my eyes narrowed in fury. "Some sort of what? Someone like me? Like my dad? Is that what you're not?" I shook my head and started to open the door, my robe in the back of his car. I didn't care. He could have it.

Tomás began to cry. "No, Olivia, no, I mean, what I meant was... please Olivia, just give me a few more minutes to explain myself," he said, looking over at me imploringly, his hand on my arm.

I shuddered violently. I would not cry. I would not let this person hold me back. I would get out of this car and I would move to New York and I would not look back. This would soon be my past, and it would be unimportant. I would joke about it in Paris, and people would laugh and we would drink champagne and I would dance and my life would be filled with magic, with crystal chandeliers and beautiful men, and expensive, all-white hotels in Rome. I felt like I was going to be sick.

"Olivia, don't you understand what I want from you?"

"Yes. You want me to go to school in New York and come back. Not to go on. You want me to come back and settle into this place that I've dedicated my life to getting out of."

"Denver is a great city. I don't know why you're always talking about getting out."

"My Denver isn't your Denver, Tomás."

"I know that. I do. But if you came back, you could dance here. What about David Taylor Dance Studio? That's a professional studio—"

"Yes, and most of the kids who go on from there, go on to New York. And the people who teach there, danced with companies based in New York."

"Olivia, I know we can figure this out. I love you. I want to have children with you."

I opened the door and stepped out. "I don't want children," I said, slamming the door.

I walked across the parking lot, holding my insides as tightly as I could. The day was warm, but night was beginning to fall. I had only brought my robe. I looked up. I was walking towards the sun as it set, towards the west, and as I walked, I was bathed in the dying light, and it covered me like my daddy's old Pendleton, and I didn't look back, in fact I didn't even think to.

Fin.

Also Available from Erika T. Wurth

Crazy Horse's Girlfriend

Indian Trains

A Thousand Horses Out to Sea